The Ladyship

By S. S. Nightshade

Paperback ISBN: 979-8-9913670-2-8

For the readers who fall in love with the

morally grey villains...

You can fix this one.

Maybe.

Trigger Warning:

The following narrative is a work of fiction and **should not be recreated in real life**. As this is a Dark Romance, it is intended for readers 18 and older.

Possible triggering elements include but are not limited to:

-domestic abuse/threats of sexual violence

-blurred consent lines

-descriptions of physical torture/PTSD

-murder and physical harm

-various uses of weapons

-explicit sexual scenes/BDSM elements

-misogynistic, sexual, and foul language

-allusions to various mental health disorders

A note from the author.

 If you made it past the trigger warning, I promise I'm not sick and twisted. *The Ladyship* was born from a re-occurring nightmare I had for about four years. The oddly specific details included an axe wielding psycho trying to kill me, on a spaceship with no power. He wore a braided lock of my hair around his wrist, but somehow I was invisible to him, so I was never actually killed in the dream.

 I decided to take a deep dive down the 'oh, what could this subconsciously mean about my life?' type of rabbit hole. What will soon be obvious, is I found a lot of things weren't as healed as I thought they were. The dark pieces, the suppressed anger, the fear that makes me freeze in place. I used this book as my release, as a way to express the weight I had on my shoulders and the chaos it created inside.

 I do want to be clear, that other than the healing and falling in love part, I am not trying to glorify any of the actions in this book. It's unhealthy. It's violent. Some parts are just downright fucked. For this reason, I want to encourage readers to take breaks if needed, and to prioritize yourselves and your needs.

 For all of my books, it's my genuine wish that my characters find special places in your hearts. And that somehow, I make the pain and mundane of our world just slightly better.

With grace, love and respect,
Nightshade

1

There were more tears on the day I was born than at some funerals.

As a child, Governess Cecelia Thorne was described as a "*perfect investment.*" Her near flawless genetics almost guaranteed the birth of a male heir, which caused many powerful men in the galaxy to barter for her hand. So many in fact, there was a literal auction for her hand in marriage.

At the ripe age of twelve, her virtue was sold to the highest bidder, Governor Arnold Thorne. As expected, she was betrothed to his only child, my father Nicholas.

After six years of courting, they were wed, and the birth of my eldest brother Xavier occurred a perfect nine months later. Over the course of the next decade, she had four more healthy sons. Samuel, Owen, Colby and finally Leonard, before the sudden death of my father.

I was a surprise. I was not supposed to happen. I was only discovered because my mother fainted at my father's funeral, blood trickling from her in a steady stream as the weight of her grief struck us both.

We were both lucky that day, in more ways than one. If her pregnancy began to show months or even weeks after his death it would have been a sure sign of scandal. The DNA test that was swiftly flown out for confirmation would have been irrefutably denied, and I would have been a bastard.

Sometimes I wish I was. I know my mother did when I was born. Because with her perfect track record, no one bothered to check the sex of the baby. Not that I, the only remainder of my father, would have been aborted anyway.

But my birth brought the end to a century's worth of peacetime, simply because I was born Alexandria instead of Alexander.

2

"It needs more green."

"Or less everything," I mutter between clenched teeth. My mother throws me an unappreciative half smile, before resuming her nonstop critique of the seamstress's work.

Despite the wrinkles etching into the corner of her eyes, and the slight flattening to her blonde curls, Governess Ceclia Thorne is still a shining jewel. All my brothers took after her, the lot of them a blonde–haired, brown–eyed wave of killer looks. She walks a slow circle around me, assessing every detail of the dress I'm stuffed into with the careful focus of a predator.

By some grace, my looks resembled my father, which helped eliminate the lingering whispers of a scandal after my birth. With my pale skin, blue eyes, and raging red hair, I was undoubtedly his. And other than the frown we both wore, looked nothing like the woman standing before me.

"Ma'am, I think we should appreciate the significance of the ceremony rather than the aesthetics." Jules, my lady's maid gently protested, pulling my attention back to the matter at hand.

"Aesthetics *are* significant, Julie." My mother chided while waving her away. She came at me with a yard of emerald satin, draping it across the waist of the tight chiffon gown. "Just look at how her hair glows. If this is to be her only public event, she must look stellar. Yes, more green indeed!" And that was that.

Jules dipped her head as the Governess exited the room without sparing me another glance.

"I think it looks great the way it is, Jules." I reach my hand towards my best friend as the door clicks shut.

"Thanks, but I know you hate it." A smile plays at the corners of her lips, but she squeezes my hand before moving back to the dress.

"Although, I think your mom could be right." She eyes the dress intensely, and I can practically see her creative mind spinning double time. She snaps her fingers, eyes brightening with an idea.

"She's probably envisioning you enveloped in every shade of green fabric I have on this ship, but adding a bit of flare to a few places like here," she lightly traces a pattern up from my hips to the sweetheart neckline, "should be enough to satisfy her, don't you think?" I suppress a chuckle, and just nod in agreement. Truthfully, I couldn't care less about it if I tried.

As Jules gets lost in her alterations, my mind drifts back to my troubled thoughts. Starting with what this dress is even for. This ceremony will be what my mother calls the 'highlight of my life', at least from a formal standpoint. Throughout my childhood she insisted I make no public appearances until the age of sixteen and told me little as to why.

For a while, I thought it was because she was ashamed of birthing me, her only female offspring, to disrupt her perfect track record. Later into my adolescence, I thought maybe she was trying to spare me from the auction pool that she was subjected to. But on my fourteenth birthday, I finally was let in on what was going on.

Simply put, my future was sealed by my family name, and my sex. My mother spent most of my life trying to hide my existence so that she could shield me from the painful truth. My brothers, Samuel especially, insisted that she thought me not knowing was one of the only ways I could grow up happily. That and the fact I was spoiled rotten.

I never was left wanting for anything. No matter how bizarre of a request I had, one of my brothers or staff members would do everything in their power to satisfy me. Clothing, technology, delicacies, and the most enthralling of all: knowledge.

I had two personal tutors who were more than willing to entertain my curiosities about our home planet, Earth. When it came to my actual studies, I was the most proficient in the subjects of history, philosophy, arithmetic and engineering, enough so that my tutors began learning from me. I know that wounded my brothers' pride, especially Xavier's, but I suppressed my own, consistently reminding them of the importance of their own roles.

Xavier has held the title of Governor since our father's passing. Dealing with the affairs of the Shiane Quadrant and its neighbors demanded his focus and attention more than his studies ever could. Shortly after his anointment, Samuel took the position of Xavier's lead advisor. His political and philosophical knowledge surpassed even mine, so he was a great asset for our brother to have.

Last year, Owen had taken over as the Quadrants treasurer, and after four years of being away Colby had graduated from the military academy and returned home. Leonard and I were just a year apart, but where I craved knowledge and participation, he seemed content with spending his days in leisure unless directly called upon.

Our mother had not yet relinquished her title and position of Governess, only at Xaviers request. Nearly two decades into his role, he was well beyond proficient at handling affairs on his own, but still relied on our mother's guiding, if not adamant, opinions. I felt a pang of guilt, knowing I also was a reason for this choice.

For years after my birth, he and my mother relentlessly studied every remaining article of the Coronation Agreement, a set of stipulations between the leading families of the Shiane Quadrant and our rival, the Gallanx Quadrant. This agreement was but a subset of the governing documents for all remaining humanity.

Six millennia ago, humans fled their dying planet, seeking refuge amongst the stars. In an effort to keep some sense of government order intact, the Coronation Treaty was written and signed by leaders of the few surviving continents.

The Treaty consisted of trade, monetary systems, areas of ownership versus opportunity, and other things affecting each of the five existing Quadrants. The Quadrants themselves wrote their own subsets called Agreements, involving how they would handle affairs individually as well as with their neighbors.

It seemed all would be well. However, despite almost being wiped off the face of existence, humans learned nothing. Without fail, we still always jumped at an opportunity to fight against one another.

From the moment the borders between the two were established, the Shiane and Gallanx Quadrants were at war. Or 'at war' as much as they could have been while floating in space light years apart. Trade deals fell through. Food was withheld. Money disappeared from accounts.

As technology became more advanced, there was the occasional drone or rocket attack against merchant vessels from passing fleets of Gallanx fighter pilots. In response, the Shiane quadrant poured the commoners' money into developing our own small fleet of pilots to intercept potential hostile ships and retaliate with our own firepower. In short, the citizens of both Quadrants were suffering terribly while the leading families wined and dined their lives away.

It took some time, but eventually the citizens banded together. In both Quadrants, people stopped working, submitting taxes, or responding to summoning's. The protests lasted thirteen years before the leading families took their citizens seriously. By then, their wealth had been drained significantly, so before the citizens became wholly independent of them, they came to an agreement.

Eight centuries ago, my ancestor Jonathan Thorne called a formal ceasefire. He and the leader of the Gallanx Quadrant, Icarus Roane, formed and added a clause to their Coronation Agreement, and that's where my bad luck came in.

The daughter of Jonathan married the son of Icarus, uniting the Quadrants forever. Despite the remaining wealth of the Shiane quadrant, the Gallanx had even more money and triple the territory. In agreement to share resources equally, resources that were hard to come by back then, the leaders of the

Shiane Quadrant agreed to gift their first-born daughters to the Gallanx leading family.

So, my fate was sealed. I was a Thorne by blood but owned by the Roanes since birth. My official debut to the Quadrants occurred two years ago at the age of sixteen. Within hours, radio messages were being sent rapid fire to my brother's office, the Roane's demanding to know when they could come to collect.

This dress my mother was so paranoid about, was for the ceremonial dinner which would take place tomorrow night. I would be on display for both Quadrants to see as I leave my home ship, *The Patron,* and board the Gallanx vessel, *The Ladyship.*

She wants me to look lovely for the cameras of course, but I think it's also for herself. So that her last memory of me would be one of shining beauty. Because odds are, once I set foot on that ship, I'll meet my end within a few hours.

The Roanes rule the most vicious of the Quadrants. In exchange for access to their weapons manufactory and skilled military task forces, they've been granted policing and disciplinary rights as determined necessary by the other leading families. Violence is sewn into their very blood. They make a living off of punishing whoever they're legally able, and then some off the record. Whatever Roane man I was gifted to would be on that vessel waiting for me, and I would be subjected to his violence.

I know I mentioned earlier that the first couple got married, but unfortunately that was one of the only happy endings between our families. There's no written stipulation in the agreement legally binding them to treat us well.

Every other gifted daughter lost their life shortly after boarding that ship. For the sake of our people, we have become sacrifices more than we are gifts. The Roanes are free to do with us as they please.

Until we die.

After final alterations, Jules stripped me of the pesky garment. To ease my building discomfort with the impending affair, we retreated to my favorite room on the ship: the library.

It held all the family treasures, of what remained of our life on Earth. Faded books with splintering spines rested in airtight cases. Faded, inky maps were displayed beneath pressed glass. One of the most fascinating things was an old compass with a cracked case, its needle spinning aimlessly in search of a North which no longer existed.

"You've been far too quiet," Jules muttered, lingering in the doorway. I hummed thoughtfully, slowly tracing my fingers across the plaster dust jackets of a few reprinted copies of books. Her face was pinched with concern, and I sighed.

"Would you rather I throw a fit? Scream and yell and tear my hair out in effort to make them not take me?"

"Yes." She said it simply, dark eyes flashing, "I'd rather you fight like hell and embarrass your family, than take this quietly." I drummed my fingers against the ancient mahogany shelves, continuing my slow circle around the room, branding it into my memory.

The blue floor lights reflected off the glass seals, casting the room into an ethereal glow. There were overhead lights of course, but I preferred the room as dark as possible. Above our heads, the ceiling opened to a portrait of the open cosmos, starlight flooding the room with enough light to read if one wanted to.

I found my gaze searching the endless expanse of space between each star. From which of these pockets of black would *The Ladyship* emerge to take me?

"I'd rather not cause more trouble. They're already enraged enough that I was hidden for so long." And threatened to blow up this ship a few times, but I didn't tell her that.

"For once, I admire your mother," Jules said. My eyes cut towards her in shock. She just shrugged nonchalantly. "She knew the risk of hiding you. Yet, she did for as long as possible to at least let you live your childhood in peace."

I hadn't thought of that before. My mother was cold, often emotionless in my presence if the situation didn't warrant a lecture. It's not as if we hated one another, but we definitely didn't have a strong relationship. Though, I couldn't ignore the merit Jules' words held. My mother, despite her lack of visible affection for me, did everything in her power over the years to keep me from this.

"If I begrudgingly agree with you," I murmured, a smile quirking on my lips, "would you feel reassured enough to leave me on my own for a while?"

Jules offered me a warm smile of her own, but I could see the sadness in it. With a dip of her head she turned, the door softly clicking shut behind her to leave me with my thoughts.

I released a long breath, eyes shifting to gaze into the glass case beside me. Within in was the small collection of Thorne Lady diaries. There were six in total, one for each of the girls who were gifted to the Roanes. They were the only thing the Roanes ever returned to us after their deaths.

The oldest belonged to Katerina, the daughter of Jonathan Thorne and the first Roane gift. The diary was at least 700 years old and looked it. Its once red cover was so faded it appeared white, and it was shriveling at the seams.

The newest diary, and I use that term lightly as it belonged to my Great Grandmother, still held its true–blue color. Across the cover, swirls of golden text glinted in the dim light, displaying the name *Julianna Thorne.*

The first five diaries contained a few notes about their experiences, or the inside layout of *The Ladyship,* but not much else of use. Majorly, they were recollections of how the initial hate and fear soon blossomed into 'romance', which really turned out to be more of relationships based on sexual benefits.

There were several lists of tips on how to woo an emotionless man, or how to use your body in your favor before he made his own plans. Each of them encouraged to make the promise of bearing a son; not that he would inherit anything. They would at least be granted a comfortable life after their mother's passing which, considering all the diaries were barely even used, came swiftly after their birth.

Julianna's book was a stark contrast to the others, and even more eerie. It was essentially completely empty, save for the first page which held just a few jotted notes of text. There was not much about her in the family records, other than she was a second—born daughter which made her gifting the first of its kind. No matter how much I dug, I couldn't find reasoning why they took her.

If she had children, that information had not been reported back to us. As usual, the only thing we had received back was this diary shortly after her passing two decades after she left. That in and of itself was a feat, as most diaries found their way back to us within the first five years. But still, she would have been just forty—eight when she died.

The mystery of it had me enraptured, and for what felt like the millionth time I found myself unlatching the case to lift it from its place. Gently, I opened the cover, eyes scanning the scant lines of text, hoping for some spark of…something. *Anything.*

November 15, 3503

The ship is large but follows the same floorplan.

Lights–out is at 14 solar hours. You will be in darkness until 24 solar hours.

No door has a lock. Barricade one to sleep so you will wake up if it is opened.

C Deck. Locker 11. Remain invisible for as long as possible.

I pursed my lips. Avoiding the Roane already aboard would be the safest course of action, especially given the families' violent tendencies. But with no locks on the doors, and with no knowledge of the ship's interior, avoidance was a temporary solution.

Perhaps this locker Julianna mentioned led to a reliable hidey hole, or a stash of items she found and used to defend herself. Whatever the case, I tucked that information away. C Deck. Locker 11. Hopefully I will be alive long enough to find it.

***

Jules was back to escort me to dinner, insisting it was "on her way" anyways. We fell into step beside each other, my worried expression hindering her usual gossipy nature.

It's not that I didn't want to enjoy these last few moments of normalcy to the fullest, I really did. But the dread settling into my bones was brewing a panic I'd rather not describe.

As we entered the dining hall Jules fell back, flanking me as a proper escort now rather than a friend. I couldn't help but worry for her, as becoming so close to me had distanced her from the rest of our other employees. Greater still, there would be no need for a lady's maid once I was gone.

All of my brothers had their own butlers, and I knew for a fact my mother would never part with Gabriella until one of them died. Xavier, knowing the depth of our bond, had promised to honor Jules' contract even if our mother was against it. But there was one small flare of hope she would be welcomed to stay for another reason.

Colby had his eyes set on Jules since we entered the room. Each of my brothers had admired her for a time, and it was easy to see why. Shining ebony hair accentuated her umber skin, and her honey brown eyes always shone with joy, if not a bit of mischief. The only thing standing in her way of securing a good match was being in my family's employ, as contracts with leading families bound the employee to our vessels for life.

Her escorting me to dinner was one of the few times she got to be in close contact with my brother. Sure enough, as soon as I was settled, Jules exited the room using the far door rather than the one we came through. And Colby had maneuvered to conveniently study the art on the wall right next to it, close enough that their fingers accidentally brushed as she passed by him into the corridor.

"The two of you are so obvious, you know that right?" I asked as soon as the door swished shut behind her. Colby's warm gaze slid to meet mine.

"I haven't the faintest clue what you're talking about."

As usual the table was already set, and together we raised our glasses to taste tonight's drink choice. The bubbles in the champagne made me giddy enough to lean forward, my voice dropping despite us being alone.

"You stopped breathing until she left the room." I smirked as he rolled his eyes, helping himself to the only bottle on the table to top off his glass.

Satisfied for now, I didn't push the subject. Unions between classes weren't all that uncommon, but with our mother? It was easy to see why they would sneak.

The door Jules exited through brushed open once more as Xavier and Samuel strode through, deep in what seemed like a heated discussion. Owen arrived a few moments later guiding our mother in by the arm, and Leonard slinked in after them like a cat. It took him all of five seconds to plop into the chair to my right and steal the rest of my champagne. Playfully, I swatted him with my napkin.

Soon Ryan, our chef, came around with the food cart and the kitchen aides brought out various more drink choices since Colby already emptied the first bottle. I smacked my lips together, eyeing the Tortellini Chicken Piccata, my favorite meal, appreciatively.

I knew my mother frowned when I leaned over to hug Ryan, whispering words of thanks. He just patted my shoulder once, wary of my mother's gaze, before moving on to serve Samuel.

As the meal progressed, conversation flowed smoothly. Not once did the Agreement come up, nor tomorrows parting banquet. In fact, I barely said a word at all. Other than receiving an occasional worried glance from one my brothers, it was like I was already gone.

4

Camera covered drones, sent by the various news and radio stations dotted throughout the Quadrants, began arriving shortly after dinner. It seemed no one was wasting any time on reporting the story of the century. Xavier immediately dismissed me to my room, the only place where I was guaranteed privacy from this point forward.

Most, if not all, of the drones had clearance to board our ship with the freedom of recording images or videos of subjects that met the keywords of their programming. These early arrivals would stockpile as much information about me as they could, in hopes of producing the most sought−after coverage about the mysterious Thorne daughter. The opportunity for a memoir about this whole affair was something my mother might even seek out herself.

More drones would be arriving tomorrow to live stream the arrival of the Roane's home vessel and *The Ladyship*, the one I was expected to board. That's why my mother was so worked up about my appearance: I would be on display to whoever in the universe would be watching. Definitely all our people, as me being gifted was the act that preserved their safety.

Aware of the cameras already seeking me out, I scurried down the corridors keeping my head bowed until the solid click of my lock slid into place. My bedroom had tempered windows, so from the outside you could only view your own disfigured reflection on a solid pane of gold.

I let my wary gaze linger on the stars beyond the tinted glass. There were no new dots of light suspended in space, or any other sign of the Roanes' approach. It was an eerie type of knowledge, knowing they were on their way but being unable to see them yet.

The ship I would be boarding was required to be stocked with everything I needed, but I *wanted* things like my leather jacket and grandfather's pocketknife. My mom hated the jacket, and she would undoubtedly burn it once I departed. Samuel hadn't a clue it was I who stole the blade, and he'd held a grudge against Owen all these years. The blade wasn't impressive, but it made me feel safer, and a bit proud.

My eyes searched my bedroom but didn't land on a single other thing I wanted to take. I didn't have to bring a diary with me, that would be waiting for me aboard the Roane ship. It was 'customary', just like that damn dress was. I blew out a huff of annoyance.

Drumming my fingers on my desk, I racked my brain for ideas on how to fight off the rising swells of anxiety and boredom. Sleep would surely not come to me tonight, so that left me with one of two things to do. I could sit in here and rot for the next eleven hours, or risk being caught by the prowling cameras and go for a walk.

I pursed my lips, deliberating my options as I crossed the room to my door. Curiously, I pressed an ear against the solid wood to see if I could pick up the dull whirr of a loitering drone, but the hallway was quiet. I cracked the door open to see all the lights dimmed and no one in sight. I closed the door.

Xavier would be furious, and my mother moved to hysterics, yet I already was back in my closet digging around in search of– found it! Snickering to myself, I dragged out a black cat suit that I wore for Halloween a few years back.

Though it was a long–forgotten celebration, my tutors were more than willing to indulge my curiosity after one of my lessons of the Home World. The costume then became one of my most adored things Jules had made me, which was why I'd kept it despite my mother's protests.

Overall, the piece was plain. The black bodysuit was made of stretchy nylon and included a now wilting tail. It was complete with a pullover hood that had a pair of kitty ears sewn onto it. Though it was one of the many things which symbolized my inability to conform, tonight it would actually serve me a great purpose.

The costume would cover everything but my face, which would hopefully confuse the drones enough to leave me alone. I zipped myself into the suit, taking the time to secure my fiery curls under the hood before cracking open my bedroom door. The coast was still clear.

Barefoot, I tiptoed down the hall with a feral kind of excitement flaring to life in my belly. Though I had much freedom, I was never one to blatantly not do as I was told. My blood pounded in my ears as I paused at the end of the corridor and peeked out into the main hallway.

Something in my chest deflated as I spotted two drones hovering about ten yards away. They were Geminis, meaning they had cameras covering each body panel. I wouldn't be able to pass without them seeing me, but if I was fast enough their programming might not recognize me.

I didn't want to hide out in my bedroom alone until my presentation. I didn't want to just sit here and wait for whatever I would be forced to accept tomorrow. And most of all, I didn't want to be just another good little Thorne girl.

I padded backwards a few steps, my heart hammering wildly in my chest. Without giving myself the time to talk myself out of it, I bolted into a full sprint. I threw my hands over my face a second before hearing a thousand clicks from the drone's cameras as I flew across the hall. I didn't dare to stop running, but a quick glance over my shoulder proved the drones didn't follow me.

I was a blur down the corridors, decidedly keeping one of my hands over my mouth and nose. Without a clear shot, most of the footage would be useless and automatically deleted.

My freedom dash was short lived. I whipped around a corner and thought I was about to screw myself by slamming into a giant drone, but a pair of arms caught me.

"What in the hell are you doing?" Colby was trying to glare at me, but I could see the corner of his mouth twitching, fighting a smile. Breathlessly, I bat my eyes at him, the picture of innocence.

"I decided not to wallow in self–pity." He released my arms with a scoff, looking like he was about to argue with me, but then Owen leaned out the door behind him.

"Why am I not shocked to already see you out here like a lunatic?" He asked me. I just grinned, and he slid into the hall next to me, wiggling his eyebrows at Colby. "What? You scared?"

"I'm not saving you from the fit mom will throw if you're caught. Either of you," Colby muttered, crossing his arms. Owen snorted as I rolled my eyes.

"Oh please. None of the drones have recognized me, otherwise a hoard of them would have followed."

"True," Colby countered, "but that doesn't mean you're making a smart choice."

"Now I didn't say that," I smirked at his look of exasperation. Before we could continue nagging one another, Owen knocked one of his hands against the wall paneling.

"Let's go Leonard. You're guilty by association by now anyways."

There was a distant groan, before Leonard joined us in the hallway. The three of us stared at Colby, until finally he gave a sigh of defeat, and pulled the door shut behind him as he joined us.

As we snuck through the ship, it was an unspoken agreement to leave Xavier and Samuel out of this. Xavier would be gutted by the press for this type of behavior, and Samuel would be so stressed out it would make the rest of us sick.

My brothers seemed content with letting me lead the way, even running as they could easily keep up. Before I knew it, Colby was locking the library doors behind us, and Owen was putting Leonard in a chokehold for stupidly reaching to turn on the lights.

The library was the furthest room from the familial quarters, so the window above us was still clear of drones. While my brothers squabbled a few feet away, I took advantage of it, lying on the floor to bathe in the starlight for what was probably the last time.

My gaze drifted across the cosmos, the vast sea of it stretching on until forever. I was calm, satiated, and utterly at peace. Until my eyes latched onto a star I had never seen before.

Suddenly, a low horn sounded, making the floor beneath me vibrate gently. Leonard and Owen quit their antics just as Colby muttered a low curse. I didn't look at them, but could feel them hovering closer. The adrenaline that still lingered in my veins evaporated and the sweat clinging to my skin sent a chill down my spine.

Perhaps it was an exploding supernova, I reasoned with myself. Or a comet passing by. It could even just be debris. Though all plausible, I knew full well who it was and why they were coming. I stood slowly, feeling a sour taste coat my tongue as I stared down the Roanes approaching vessels.

My mind told me I should be afraid,
but all that resonated within my shaking
fingertips, was rage.

The Thornes home vessel was more impressive than I imagined it in my head. I knew they were a wealthy family but, given the stories, I always figured they couldn't hold a candle to us. As we approached, I studied its exterior from my place on the bridge of *The Piston*. It was clear at least some of my assumptions were wrong.

For a ship its size, I could tell it was quick. I noted that it was outfitted with three gunner stations, two on the top and one on the belly. It also seemed to be equipped with a deflector shield, most likely meant for stray meteorites. And the way it shone; I'd be willing to bet the damn thing was reinforced with an alloy containing raw diamond.

It would take more than a couple of our rockets to break the thing, let alone blow it to pieces. Still, I was tempted to try. I knew which window was Her's after all, and the obnoxious gold pane made a tantalizing target.

The Ladyship was being towed below us, the old, blackened steel thing making us travel twenty something clicks slower than I preferred. I didn't know the name of the Thorne home ship. I didn't care. I didn't care for this entire thing to begin with.

The first thing I would do when I saw her would be punish her for failing to keep herself hidden and dragging us both into this bullshit of a mess. Hell, if it weren't for her, I wouldn't have been forced back into military training for a third time.

The first time was customary, my duty as a Roane to prepare myself physically and mentally to defend our people and uphold our values: strength, and conquest. These two aspects were the only things which kept humanity alive for this long. So, at freshly thirteen, I was shipped off for a year and half.

Back then, the drills and the tests pushed all the physical and mental barriers a child would have. And the graduation ceremony, if it could be called that, would be my first taste of my father's real expectations of me. I was not discharged until I could prove I was independently capable of ending a life when the situation demanded it. It took me executing four convicts within a minute to prove that feat.

The second round of training was split into two eight—month segments. The first was less hands on, focusing more on specialized skills: tactical weapons and movement, space flight, invasion tactics, and the like. The second segment focused on the art of torture. Again, on criminals, some of the worst we picked up in our Quadrant as well as others. So, in a way, my actions were justified.

After a time, I began finding it easy to unleash physical pain on another. Flaying a man's skin off his bones became busy work. After all, he kidnapped girls and bred them, just to sell their male children as soon as they were done breastfeeding to the highest bidder. My pent—up adolescent resentment toward my emotionally absent mother, enjoyed slowly sawing the hands off of women who abused, neglected, or dared to abandon their own kids.

But my personal favorite, was when I would get to unleash the growing monster inside me on a blue blood like myself. One who thought their money and prestige equaled power. I damn near loved reminding them who had the actual power. With them I'd take my time, starting with their fingernails and finishing with their teeth, watching the fight drain from them and be replaced by despair as they realized their cash couldn't satiate my wrath.

Up until that point, I was a naïve fool to believe in people, to seek out the good in them. That round of training proved to me just how monstrous the human race is, and what lengths a person will go to if driven by greed. And how much further they would go if they got off on the pain they caused.

But the third round of training, everything changed. There was nothing else for me to be taught; I had become the destructive force my father expected me to be. So instead of giving me a blade, he forced me under it.

For a year, I was locked up alongside the prisoners I had previously overseen breaking. They took great advantage of the opportunity; I was beaten in my sleep so many times I began dozing outside the guard's office during rec time. Then I'd stay up all night, waiting for who would sneak into my cell to shank me in my sleep. I was the only one who got away with murder in prison.

But the worst was the year after that. After my nerves were shot, my body malnourished and my brain rewired from prison life, I was dragged into the same torcher chambers where I used to practice my skills on the convicts. The memories of that time were fuzzy, but the fishbowl sense of quiet which would be followed by agonizing bouts of pain never failed to fade.

When I'd come to, usually with blood still pouring from a fresh wound, I wouldn't be bound anymore and there would be a weapon on the floor in front of me. Sometimes a gun, sometimes a knife, sometimes a club. And chained across from me, would be some random person.

They were never convicts. Turns out, my father had his men kidnap them for me to practice all I'd learned on. If I didn't kill them, my father's men would come in and force me to watch what they'd do to them.

It took a dozen people getting tortured or raped while being starved to death a few feet away, for me to finally snap. As soon as I would wake with a new person, I'd kill them with whatever weapon I was provided. I considered them mercy killings, for it was far faster than what the others would do to them.

At first this pleased my father. My own torture lessened, as did the number of people he would bring before me to kill. But then he demanded me to drag it out, to take hours, sometimes days, to kill them, just as I had with the convicts. The weapons were no longer provided, and I had to start killing them with my bare hands. And the one time I dared refuse, turning the blade on his men instead...

The Piston shuddered as we came to a sudden halt beside the Thorne vessel. The momentum carried me forward quick enough to literally jerk me out of the memories threatening to break me from the inside. My hand came up to smack against the glass, keeping me upright as I felt a second shudder rock the floor as we docked.

I ignored the dull throb on the side of my face, that particular memory itching too close for comfort. Shoving off the glass, I began stalking back to my room.

As I went, the servants practically fled out of my way. It made sense. When I got back six months ago, my father took things one step further, and had me practice my skills on them at random. He insisted that I needed to be well versed in the real thing, but I think it was just his way of passing the time until today. Or confirm that I was thoroughly brainwashed.

But I wasn't. I still felt their blood on my hands, and heard their screams echo in my ears. Even now, I felt the sick wave of guilt rolling through me as Adam, one of the chef assistants, froze down the hallway ahead of me.

Just last week, I had gutted his twin brother, Christian. Adam had been on the other side of the door begging and screaming for me to stop, but I didn't. What was left of his twin's body now floated somewhere in the dead vacuum of space behind us.

She would die just for that.

6

I had enough sense to return to my room well before the Roane vessels docked beside *The Patron*. As expected, sleep evaded me, so I just watched their slow approach until the view from my room was completely obscured by *The Ladyship*.

This would be my new home, until I died... or escaped. I pushed that thought from my mind, unwilling to entertain the fantasy any longer. They were here. There was no stopping it now. And to make it worse, a prickly voice from my subconscious decided it was appropriate to whisper the idea that they were blocking my window on purpose.

Part of me wondered if it was even safe, as it looked centuries old. I didn't even see an addition on the hull to house the mechanism for a modern deflector shield. Perhaps a comet smashing into it would kill me before the man waiting for me on it would.

By the time Jules entered my chambers the next solar morning, I had showered three times, already feeling unclean. I was plucked and preened for what felt like hours. That combined with my mounting panic had me on the verge of smacking Jules when she sinched my corset too tight. I tried distracting myself by focusing on the new details of the dress, trying to appreciate my friend's work.

I couldn't argue that it was a beautiful thing. Instead of adding green fabric, she encrusted shattered pieces of emerald atop the soft white neckline. The skirt, however, was wholly replaced by the emerald silk my mother had chosen, and was accented with thin strips of pure white lace running down the length of my legs. I felt a pang of guilt as I realized she was probably up all night sewing.

My mother wanted my hair straightened and plastered to my head. I didn't even want to brush it. Jules helped us find common ground on tamed waves. Which of course, just had to be pinned back from my face with about seven hundred silver clips.

I looked stunning. I looked tempting. I did not look like myself at all. I ceased caring as soon as I had a drink in my hand.

"I really wish you had waited to be served champagne at dinner," my mother hissed as she fiddled with last minute adjustments on her own gown. She was in a floor length sapphire blue number, which complemented her perfect blonde hair and perfect brown eyes just freaking perfectly. I slapped my empty glass down on a passing tray.

"Ever hear of the term liquid courage, mother?"

"How many times have I told you not to mutter?" She deflected, raising one of her delicate brows. I rolled my eyes.

"I shall wait for my next glass to be served at the table. Satisfied?" She gave me a curt nod before holding me at arm's length, eyes traveling up and down me one more time. I was shocked to see tears brimming when she met my gaze again.

"Alexandria, I know this isn't what you want. But sometimes arranged unions, even ones in severe circumstances–"

"You're right," I cut her off, more venom seeping into my voice than I meant as I added, "It's not what I want, but that's rarely mattered to you, hasn't it?"

Her expression went blank, and she dropped her hands back to her sides. For a moment she looked wounded, but then she took a quick, deep breath and her gaze hardened once more.

"Please wait for your brother to escort you in. We need to make an extra effort to keep our appearances intact after your jaunt through the ship last night."

She slipped through the dining hall door as my mouth dropped open in shock. Here I was, about to be handed over to a home-grown serial killer, and still her biggest concern was appearances. I shouldn't have been shocked.

I paced in the corridor, resisting the urge to shout for a servant to refill my glass. The minutes ticked by like hours until, mercifully, Xavier finally appeared at the end of the corridor.

I was shocked to see him in his public affairs tuxedo, the gold and navy-blue clashing severely with the shade of my dress.

"Well look at that, you actually waited," he teased by way of greeting. I resisted every fiber of my being which wanted to roll my eyes.

"Yes, well. Mother made it clear I already damaged our reputation enough last night by daring to walk around on my own ship."

"I don't think she would have been bothered by it if not for that costume you wore," Xavier said with a heavy sigh.

I winced. Though I had covered my face well, it didn't even cross my mind that the skintight costume would clearly show my figure.

"Would you believe it was actually Mother having a mental breakdown?" I asked, feigning innocence.

"You sell that story to any newsroom, and I'll make you the Governor of our quadrant myself." He grinned and offered me his arm. At my pause he finally met my gaze, voice softening as he said, "I want to assure you, I did everything I could to try and get you out of this. I'm sorry that I failed you."

Some of the anger in me ebbed, my heart aching to see him blaming himself. Xavier was always the strong one, the one who never failed, the one who never lost control when the rest of us were spiraling, but now here we were, whispering in a hallway about to be torn away from one another.

I opened my mouth, searching for reassurances I didn't have, but he held up a hand stopping me. He took a half step forward, wrapping me in his arms. His grip on me was tight, safe. "I tried. I really did try," he murmured, voice breaking.

I can't remember the last time any of my brothers, let alone my mother, hugged me. The suddenness of it had tears springing from my eyes, and I suppressed a sob against his chest.

"I don't want to go," I admitted, "I'm afraid."

"You are a Thorne, Alexandria. And you are the brightest of us all, so I trust you'll understand the meaning of what I say next."

Xavier eased me back, gloved hands gently wiping at my cheeks, doing his best not to smudge my makeup further. His eyes bore into mine, the emotion in them a stark contrast to my mother's empty gaze. He held me by the shoulders as he said,

"You exist beside the flower, but you are not its weak petals. You my sister, can draw blood."

7

I was under the impression that only Xavier would be escorting me in, but it seems my brothers came up with their own plans. Samuel, Owen, Colby and Leonard, all dressed in their public affairs suits, were waiting for us just inside the door. They flanked Xavier and I on either side as soon as we entered. Immediately, I felt less exposed to the eyes and cameras peering at me from all angles.

Hundreds of drones lined the edges of dining hall, stacked atop one another five rows deep. Other than our Mother, there were only three more guests seated at the table, but it might as well have been an army.

Richard and Tabitha Roane sat side by side at the head of our table in the space we usually left empty for our Father. I immediately felt Xavier stiffen as he registered this, but ever the diplomat, he just met their judgmental stares with a warm smile. Meanwhile, I wanted to take my heels off and gouge their eyes out with them.

Beside them on their right was who I assumed was their youngest son, Jetson. I had heard of him numerous times on the radio each solar Friday, and it was never for positive reasons.

The three of them were a wall of steely black shadows, from their clothes to their hair. Intimidating and impenetrable. I gripped my brother's arm tighter before lowering myself into my seat.

As soon as my glass was filled, I raised it to my lips, downing a long, slow gulp in hopes to quell my anxiety. I focused on breathing evenly and remaining poised, centering on the music that had started up from the far end of the dining hall. There was a flute, a violin, and was that a harp perhaps?

"So, Alexandria." Automatically, I straightened in my seat, eyes drifting to find Richard's intense gaze on me. His voice, like his presence, was heavy and cold. He smirked at me, as if humored by my immediate attention before saying, "Tell me about yourself. I'm very interested to know all about my lovely daughter–in–law."

Silver screeched against chinaware as everyone froze. Even the musicians jarred their next few notes in shock before continuing on in a pathetic attempt to make this dinner seem graceful. Out of the corner of my eye, I noticed Tabitha jerk her head to look at her husband, as if she was just as surprised by the title he addressed me with as the rest of us were.

Stalling, I raised my glass to my lips again, wondering what type of trick he was playing at. Did he watch the footage from last night and plan to humiliate me with it? Or was he making an opening for polite conversation for the drones to eat up?

Citizens from both Quadrants were watching, and I was a mystery to every single one of them. But instinctively I knew that there was no way his curiosity was sincere.

I lowered my now empty glass, flashing a practiced smile towards him. When I spoke, my voice was the epitome of a proper, elegant lady.

"I'm sincerely touched by your interest. It makes me have hope for our families as we honor the treaty." My fingertip traced the rim of my glass, my eyes never leaving his as I added, "As for me, I guess the most intriguing thing you'll find is my spirit."

He blinked, the only sign that I touched a nerve. Honestly, I wasn't a bit surprised. He was the most powerful and dangerous man across the stars, but I was the one thing he couldn't obtain, destroy, or force into submission. He gave that up by not being the man waiting for me aboard *The Ladyship,* and judging by the fury now edging his gaze at my choice of words, he regretted that decision heavily.

I received a quick, dismissive flick of his hand, and barely contained my smug grin as the clicking from the drones' cameras reached my ears. Their presence was the only thing keeping me cemented in the gravity of the situation. If Richard was this intimidating just to speak to and I wasn't even his gift, I didn't want to imagine what the man aboard *The Ladyship* was like.

Now, Richard turned all of his attention to Xavier and my Mother. His new source of entertainment seemed to be landing politically correct blows on them. A wave of guilt crept through me as I watched them struggle to keep a higher ground. I was the one who pissed him off, but they were getting the heat for it.

Without warning, Jetson smacked his hand down on the table, and the sudden noise made me flinch in my seat. Everyone, even his father, fell silent as he lifted his fork, pointing it towards me.

"I want another look at her. Get up."

At this point, I was unsure if it was the champagne on an empty stomach or my nerves serrating my braincells, but the cheery music in the background made his demand almost comical to me. Before I could say anything stupid though, my Mother's voice was ringing gently in my ears next.

"I'm sorry, what are you asking?" She ventured carefully, dipping her head to the side casually as if this were a pleasant conversation. Jetson didn't bother masking his disgust before turning back to me, mouth splitting into a twisted grin.

"That cat suit she had on last night did better things for her figure than this dress." I felt my face flush with embarrassment, but he just plowed on, "Plus, can we even be sure this is her and not some type of trick? Surely the cameras would have captured that wild red hair of hers?"

"I assure you we are playing no tricks." Xavier's voice was hard as iron as he ground out, "My only sister sits before you, and I will not allow you to insult her while she remains on this ship."

Jetson's smile grew sinister.

"I'll say whatever I damn well please about her, and you should mind your place, Thorne. She belongs to us now."

A low laugh sounded from behind me, instantly wiping the grin right off Jetson's face and halting the music. The only sounds in the room were the rapid fire clicking of the drones' cameras, and the heavy thud of bootsteps approaching my back.

"That's only somewhat correct brother."

The male voice above my head was somehow both terrifyingly low and reassuringly soft. I felt his weight lean against the back of my chair, and goosebumps peppered my skin as his hand came over my shoulder to gently close around my throat.

I stopped breathing entirely as his thumb caressed my pulse and that voice whispered right into my ear,

"She belongs to *me*."

8

The dining room erupted.

Simultaneously, Xavier and Richard stood from their seats, the former rounding the table to yank me out of my chair. Richard's face was red with rage, his finger pointing at the man who was still casually braced against the back of my chair. The man who I could only assume was Braxon Roane.

Like his family, he wore all black, though his leather jacket and jeans were a far cry from the formal wear the rest of us donned. His face was downcast, shoulder length hair hanging like a steel curtain between me and any features I could hope to see.

"It is customary for you not to see your bride until aboard the vessel!" Richard's voice boomed through the room like thunder, causing the crystal tableware to rattle.

Braxon flexed his hands against the headrest of my abandoned seat and scoffed.

"Well, she threw that custom to hell last night." Though he was clearly as aggravated as his father was, I swore I could detect an underlying note of humor in his statement.

A new wave of embarrassment tore through me as I realized he was referring to my cat costume as well. Unlike his brother, he continued without further comments on my figure, "Besides, I at least took precaution to maintain some type of decorum."

I held my breath as he finally straightened and turned towards me- and was instantly annoyed. A black mask covered the lower half of his face, revealing nothing to me but copper skin and slate-grey eyes. It was impossible to tell how old he was, but judging from the lack of wrinkles on his forehead and crisp black hair, I assumed he was on the younger side. I was too busy gawking at him to realize he had asked me a question, until Xaviers grip on my arm tightened a degree.

"I'm sorry, what?" I received a series of looks ranging from flabbergasted to outraged, but all Braxon did was grunt before repeating,

"I asked why you were dressed like a doll when it's clearly not your style." I couldn't help but frown, my annoyance flaring.

"Would you rather I be here in the catsuit?"

"Alexandria!" My mother hissed, her voice pitching in warning, but I didn't avert my gaze from Braxon's. He looked at me coldly, assessing, and perhaps slightly intrigued.

"If I ordered you to change into it, would you?" I swear he smirked under the mask.

"No." My voice was flat, and defiant.

I heard Jetson rise from the table, but a single glare from his brother had him back in his seat. Slowly, Braxon crossed the space Xavier had put between us, giving my brother a pointed look over my shoulder to not interfere.

My hands were trembling with the effort to not reach up and smack him as he paused in front of me, completely invading my space. I refused to step back, ignoring the ache in my neck as I bent my head back to stare up into his eyes. We were so close that when I crossed my arms they brushed against his jacket.

"You're a fiery little thing, aren't you Red?" His voice was hushed, the mask making him barely audible. I cocked my head.

"Red?"

He nodded, reaching for me again, and I stiffened as his fingers slowly plucked all the silver clasps from my hair and dropped them to the floor. Despite being securely tied into my gown's corset, I felt stripped naked as he shook my curls free, fingers lingering on the ends of my hair as he turned away from me.

"Dinners over. Load her things on *The Ladyship* and see to it she boards in 30 minutes or less."

"What!?" I jumped away from him, Xaviers' hand grabbing mine again and restoring the distance between me and Braxon. His voice held an edge of fear now as he began to argue.

"It's customary for the bride to spend the night on her own ship and board come solar mor–"

"She threw custom out the window with her own behavior last night." Braxon cut off my brother with a growl, "'As soon as their eyes meet, she's given.' That's what the agreement says, and she just spent an awful long time looking right at me. It's done. She's mine. And I'll blow your ship to smithereens if you don't hand her over."

He didn't so much as spare me a second glance as he stalked from the room. Jetson was doubled over with laughter, and Richard looked quite pleased with how things turned out. The clicking of the drones' cameras were beginning to make me dizzy as the weight of what just happened hit me.

Desperately, I looked across the table to Samuel, but he was crouched in front of our Mother, hiding her face in his chest as her shoulders shook. Colby was standing behind them, glaring at the Roanes with an intensity which rivaled the one Braxon gave his brother just moments before. Owen was full on grabbing drones, practically throwing them out the door after Braxon, but it was Leonard who walked up to me and took my free hand.

With a gentle pull, he guided me away from Xaviers' side, away from the cameras, and into the kitchen. I gasped for a breath in the sudden quiet, stumbling ahead of him to hurl up the champagne I'd drank into the sink. His hand rubbed gentle circles on my back as I braced myself on the sinks edge, shuddering against the crashing waves of fear and rage.

The treaty's agreement had never once been altered or updated. According to it, I had been given. And if I resisted, they would kill us all.

***

Leonard led me back to the familial quarters through the ships servants' passageways to avoid any lingering drones. Most would be heading outside by now to capture my crossing to *The Ladyship,* but after what just transpired there would still be a few on board to capture every last detail of my life.

Jules burst into the hallway ahead of us, the frantic look on her face replaced by a more controlled sense of worry as soon as our eyes locked. She said nothing, replacing Leonard at my side as he paused at the door she had just come through. He leveled a rare, serious gaze at me.

"We've got this handled here Alex," he said, "take everything you want or need, even shit from our rooms. I'll take the heat for it."

"The ship should have everything I need on it already," I replied, my voice sounding airy even in my ears.

"Alex," Leonard gripped my shoulders tightly, pulling me out of my daze. "We will be fine."

I nodded once, feeling tears brimming in my eyes as I realized this would be the only goodbye I would get to have. There wasn't enough time.

Leonard's arms wrapped around me then, hugging me tight enough to crush the air from my lungs but I savored the feeling. When he pulled back, his gaze locked on mine again. "Now go kick his ass."

I didn't let myself break beneath the burst of pain in my chest when the door shut between us, just turned back toward Jules to hurry toward my room. As we went, I focused on my breathing, and focused on my anger. I didn't have time to cry right now. To protect my family, I needed to get on that ship.

I threw open the door to the main hallway, hand coming up to shield my eyes against the flashing cameras on the drones littering the corridor. I stalked across the few feet to my bedroom door, yanking it open just wide enough for Jules to squeeze in behind me before slamming it against the cameras as hard as I could.

"I can't believe that just happened." Jules's voice was shaking slightly.

"Neither can I," I murmured, staring out my window at the damn ship loitering there. "One of Colby's old duffle bags is in my closet. Stuff it with t-shirts, tanks, leggings, all things comfortable and plain. I don't plan on wearing anything Braxon's provided."

She nodded once, scurrying to the closet to retrieve the bag. As she folded the clothing I requested, I pried open the secret compartment under my desk and fished out my grandfather's pocketknife. It was small in size but would be coming with me. And right now, it served a greater purpose.

Jules whipped around at the sound of tearing fabric, eyes widening in horror as she watched me cut my way out of the dress she had crafted.

"I'm sorry," I said, and I meant it. "I can't parade myself out there in this, and I can't leave it in a state where it's an option." Tears pricked her eyes, but she nodded in agreement.

While she continued to pack my clothes, I retrieved the small backpack from my school days and went to the bathroom to stuff it with all my toiletries. When I returned to her side, we quickly added all my socks and underwear to the bag and a few pairs of sneakers. Fuck the bras.

"Is there anything else you would like to bring?" Jules's voice was quiet, and I could hear her sniffle.

I thought of all the books in the library, and the view I would never see again. Of my brothers, whose last memories of me would be tinged with panic. And Jules, my best friend. I turned to her, wrapping her in my arms.

"I'm sorry we won't have a proper goodbye," I whispered as she hugged me back tightly. "Because I really need you to go get Great Grandmother Juliannas journal from the library. She wrote things in it I'll need, and I don't have time to get changed and get across the ship and back before crossing."

She was already nodding her head as she pulled back from my embrace. After swiping the few tears from her eyes, she turned back to the door, almost slipping on the discarded tatters of the dress on the floor.

"What on earth are you going to wear?" She whispered, shaking her head with a short chuckle. I mustered a grin for her before lifting the knife again, this time using it to cut the lacing of my chemise.

"Something way better than the catsuit."

'No.'

It had taken all my willpower to not stumble back in shock from a single word. Her defiance burned like acid, and I'd wanted to smack her for it. After her stunt last night, I expected her to be reserved, if not terrified, by my sudden presence. Surely, she knew what to expect when she got on that ship?

Jetson fell in step beside me, going on and on about how he would have bent her over the table in front of all those cameras to teach her a lesson about respect. A piece of me withered at the look of pure glee in his eyes.

My brother was naturally what our father forcibly created in me. Brutal, and devilish. I had little doubt that if our roles were reversed and he had gotten her, she wouldn't have lasted long. Not that I'm going to make it pleasant for her.

Of course, she had to be beautiful. I had her single debutant photo from two years ago, but it was horrific. There was more makeup on her face in that image than probably existed in some parts of her quadrant. The pristine girl smiling at the camera was a far cry from her true self, I could tell that just by watching the videos of her last night.

And Jetson was right. That damn catsuit did nothing to hide her curves, and it pissed me off to all hell when I realized I had gotten hard just from watching her. Even more annoyingly, her face was always blurred in the dark, half covered by the hood or her hands. I must have watched over twenty different videos of her before giving up and going to bed.

I wasn't prepared to see her in person—I wasn't prepared for *her* at all. Of course, she stood out physically with that brilliant red hair. It was long enough to swish against her hips, which were sinched wickedly tight by her corset. But it was the way she refused to back down, going head-to-head with me in that room which made my dick nearly spring out of my pants. And that voice; sharp yet lovely. Like a blade.

Roughly, I shook my head, wiping my hands down the front of my jeans. Hands that had been stained with innocent blood, because of her. Resolved by that fact, I tuned back in to what my brother was saying, but instantly wished I hadn't.

"So how long do you plan to toy with her?" Jetson's voice in my ear lowered a degree, his eyes flashing with a predatory gleam. "You better at least fuck her first, otherwise it's a waste."

I halted and dropped my hand onto his shoulder, fingers digging in just slightly. It was an effort to keep from showing my disgust, but I mastered myself enough to keep my voice carefully neutral and my gaze razor sharp.

"If you share any more opinions about what I should do to her, I'll start testing those methods on you." He grinned at me, like it was a secret promise and not a threat.

"Careful, Braxon. Do you want to look like you fancy the bitch in front of the cameras?" I had completely forgotten about the drones. With a curse, I released my brother.

"Don't get the wrong idea. Just because I don't jerk off while watching people get waterboarded like you do, doesn't mean I have anything sweet planned for her."

"That's why I'm offering my creative services, brother." If possible, his grin grew wider, "Father taught you how to end her. But we both know it could be so much more fun for you, if you just explore what itches you want to have scratched."

I stifled a sigh as we entered the flight deck. Typically, when moving from one vessel to another the travelers would don a space suit and use a handheld, magnetic catapult to swing from one ship to the other. This, however, was a special occasion.

Both flight decks of the ships were aligned, and a long, titanium walkway connected the bridge of the Thorne vessel to the bridge of *The Ladyship*. The entire walkway was suspended in an airlock that had been constructed piece by piece over the course of the past several hours.

The design was so that she could make a dramatic entrance, one that was camera worthy, and cross the bridge from her vessel to mine while smiling and waving to the surrounding drones like a princess. Personally, I just wanted to stuff her in a space suit and chuck her aboard, but my mother insisted on giving her a 'proper entrance' as dictated by the treaty.

I started for the walkway, wanting to get off this ship as fast as possible, but this time Jetson smacked his palm down on my shoulder.

"Are you going to bother saying goodbye to mother and father?" His eyes had lost their manic gleam and were coolly assessing me now. Apparently, I hadn't played along very well.

"I already gave mother my farewells." That was true.

Though her absence in my childhood was still wedged between us like a knife, as I aged, I understood her distance. As the eldest son, I wasn't permitted such childish things as having my mother around. It would make me weak; reliant. Before my first round of training, she only spoke to me when necessary, and saw me even less. In fact, since my return six months ago, we've spoken more than we did in my entire life.

After all I'd been through, something in me sympathized with her. I mean shit, look at the family she married into. If I had a child, knowing they would grow up to become a monster no matter what I did, I probably wouldn't put much effort into loving them either.

As for my father, I didn't plan on seeing him again at all, even after all this was over. As soon as I was on that ship, custom demanded the only one who could board was the gifted Thorne. My family would remain on *The Piston* until I returned.

But the agreement never dictated that I must. That was the small loop of freedom this shit show could give me, if I just got it over with. Noticing the shift in my demeanor, Jetson released his grip on me and nonchalantly slid his hands into his pockets and grinned.

"Don't have too much fun without me, brother. I'll give Father your regards." I didn't bother telling him to leave out that last part as he sauntered away, back down towards the airlock to join our parents. I didn't mull over it any longer, turning on my heel to cross to *The Ladyship*.

Thousands of drones, news and personal, were already finding their places in a full 360 of the walkway, recording and reporting on my every step. The headlines tomorrow would blast the Roane family about my inappropriate appearance, both timing and outfit wise, and a darkness in me was pleased by that idea. I chuckled under the mask as I crossed the bridge to enter the captain's office, but halted in the doorway.

Surely the servants didn't misinterpret my orders and delivered her belongings to a different part of the ship? I was expecting to find bag upon bag stuffed to the brim with all her belongings that I could do what I pleased with, but the office was empty. There was nothing to destroy, nothing to launch into space, nothing to manipulate

her with or get her to beg. Before my rage
could simmer into flame, the deafening
thunder of a thousand cameras behind me
made me whip around.

I was grateful the mask hid my jaw as
it dropped to the floor, but the smirk on her
face told me she knew. She stood in the
center of the walkway with a small backpack
hanging from her shoulders and a duffle bag
clenched tightly in one fist. Her outfit was
definitely not meant for a woman of her
prestige: faded black boots, ripped black
jeans, and a leather jacket infuriatingly
similar to mine.

Her hair fell in wild red curls, and the
near feral glint in those sapphire eyes gave
me the sudden urge to yank it. Before I could
muster a reaction, she raised her free hand
and did something that actually made me
choke.

There, in front of our families, in front
of the drones broadcasting us to the entire

universe, she smiled and flipped her middle finger up, right at me.

Never mind what I expected from tomorrow's headlines. She just guaranteed they would all be about her.

10

Braxon didn't look at me or touch me as I quickly shuffled past him onto the ship. Luckily, he seemed just as keen as I was on the broadcast ending as soon as possible. As soon as the door sealed shut behind me, he ducked back into the captain's room with barely a glance. I'm assuming to prepare the ship for departure. I didn't stick around to find out what he had in store for me.

Julianna's diary said none of the doors on the vessel had a lock. While that was dangerous, it also meant I had as much freedom and few restrictions as he did.

I strode across the entry deck, the dark red carpet making my footfalls near soundless. I wrinkled my nose, not letting my mind drift to *why* they chose red. Definitely not thinking that it would help hide blood stains. Nope, not going there. Pausing before the only other door, I took a breath, flexed my shaking fingers, and flung it open.

I found myself standing in a kitchen. The appliances were clearly dated, but functional. Like the deck behind me, the floor was red, shifting to tile for functionality. Maneuvering around the island, I approached the next door. I wanted to get as far from the captain's office as possible, at the very least off the same deck while time was on my side.

Quickly, I passed through the remaining rooms. There was a planetarium with a full glass ceiling, and it had a full bathroom tucked into the back corner. To my pleasant surprise, the next door opened up to a library. It was an effort not to pause, my curious mind already buzzing at the prospect of having new material to read and study. The last room was an entertainment space, complete with a pool table and home theater. On the far wall was what appeared to be an elevator to go down to the next deck.

I didn't trust it to work. Like most of the other mechanical features, it looked over a century old. Plus, getting trapped in there with Braxon was not high on my to do list. Luckily, there was a servant's stairwell halfway hidden behind a pinball machine. I dipped inside, shutting the door firmly behind me, before sitting on the top step and gasping in a breath.

I had no idea how many decks this ship had, but if I had to guess, I would say at least five. If I remember correctly, one of the Thorne diaries stated the floorplan on each deck was the same. That would mean there were five different rooms on each deck, plus a bathroom in the middle. So at least twenty-five rooms in all; surely, I could avoid my keeper.

Quickly, I pulled out Julianna's diary and a pen to scribble down the layout of the top deck. I hoped there was more than just this stairwell and the elevator to travel between decks.

I flipped back a page, studying the short lines of advice my great grandmother bothered to leave for the next Thorne girl. I tapped the fifth line.

C deck. Locker 11. I needed to know why she was so specific about that, and sooner rather than later.

A crackle of static overhead interrupted my thoughts, and instinctively I pressed my back into the wall trying to become smaller. After a few more pops and fizzes, the static faded into deafening silence.

"I hope you chose a good hiding spot Red." Braxon's voice drifted down to me, deep and foreboding.

"Bastard," I muttered, getting to my feet once more.

"That's not how to address your master, now is it?"

I stumbled, bracing my hands on the railing. Was this guy for real? But more importantly, how did he hear me?

I glanced back the way I'd come, eyes searching for him, but I was alone. The speakers were constantly popping with static interference, but it did nothing to dampen his sadistic laugh. A sheen of sweat coated my skin, but I forced my shaking legs to keep moving.

"The speakers are two-way, Red." My heart thundered in my ears as he explained, "I can hear everything you say. I can hear you cry. I can probably even hear your breath if I adjust the settings enough."

"That's one way to say you're obsessed with me," I muttered, taking the stairs two at a time. I flew past the entrance to B deck, before flinging open the door to C deck. He barked out a laugh.

"Just reminding you that you can't hide, although I invite you to try. This would be boring otherwise." That comment made me pause just inside the doorway.

Should I be boring? If I was dull, he'd end it quickly, and maybe avoid some of the more brutal things he had planned for me. My shaking hands grew steady, curling into fists at the thought. I squeezed my eyes shut, forcing myself to inhale deeply, to curb my ever-brewing rage into resolve. I was gonna fight like hell, even if it was stupid.

I peered around the room, not daring to look for a light switch in case there were cameras. It looked like a studio of some kind, with boxes and sound equipment stacked as high as the ceiling. Carefully, I wove through the maze, trying to prevent knocking anything over before opening the next door.

Now this looked promising. The room housed several different machines, and had an entire wall covered in mirrors; clearly it was a home gym. The space was double the size of the other rooms, so if the layout upstairs held true, the next set of doors should lead to a bathroom. I broke into a jog, swinging the door open and stepping into what looked like an old-fashioned locker room. Jackpot!

My momentary triumph quickly deflated when I realized there were no numbers on the lockers. I scanned the two rows, both painted a faded blue, the dented metal doors barely holding shut. If I had to count, did I need to go clockwise? Counterclockwise?

"That's an interesting choice," Braxon's voice interrupted my thoughts, "of all rooms to pick to camp out in, I mean."

I stopped breathing, "How do you know what room I'm in?" He didn't respond for several seconds and, stupidly, I thought I might have called his bluff. But then he snickered.

"Whenever you open a door, a notification gets sent to my handheld." The locker room door behind me swung open with a bang and I whipped around.

His jacket was gone, and his black T-shirt did nothing to hide his hulking body corded with muscles. But it wasn't his physique which made my eyes widen– it was the axe resting atop his shoulder.

"I might not be able to see you," he said, voice laced with dark laughter, "but I'll always know exactly where you are."

11

Her attitude alone was going to make me kill her. I assumed she would probably talk to herself in a panic, or try to encourage herself to not give up hope, but again she took me by surprise. So why the hell shouldn't I surprise her right back?

As I retrieved my axe from B deck, I kept talking to keep her distracted. I'd essentially turned the one room into a weapons vault, and part of me now wondered if that was a wise choice. Given her temper, I wouldn't put it past her to steal something from in here to use against me. Luckily, I'd locked the firearms in individual cases, so she wouldn't be able to shoot me in my sleep.

I gave the axe a swing, the worn leather handle settling in my grip like a second skin. I'd acquired the weapon during my first bout of military school. It was by no means the most impressive in my collection, but it was simple and never failed to get the job done.

The blade was an eye-catching red, and cut to mimic that of a firefighter's. Though the profession died out since humanities transition to space, it was immortalized and revered. Given the reputation of the weapon's usual wielder, it made me feel less evil when I was 'at work.'

The look on her face when she saw it was priceless. It was a mixture of shock, fear, and yet still some annoyance tinted the depths of her eyes. Finally, she dropped the damn bags she was carrying and made a break for it through the opposite doors. I sighed.

"Oh sweetheart, don't you want to try and get to know each other?" I asked, sauntering after her. There was a moment of silence before her voice sliced through the speaker overhead.

"Sure, what's your favorite color?

I laughed out loud. Despite running away, and the pure terror in her voice, she still had that fire in her.

"Red," I ducked into a hidden entrance behind the last locker, which housed the remnants of an old spiral staircase. "But I'm guessing you already knew that."

Her answering huff was full of exasperation. I checked the handheld in my pocket, the sensor for one of D deck's entrances lighting up the screen. I grinned. This was about to get *really* interesting.

I took the stairs two at a time, planning to catch up to her before she could flee the room she was about to barge into. I threw open the hidden door, emerging from the backside of a floor-to-ceiling mirror in the bathroom. Not bothering to shut it behind me, I kicked open the bathroom door to see her frozen in the center of the room. She wasn't looking at me and that didn't come as a surprise.

"I see you've found the dungeon."

Her widened eyes drifted across the rows of glass display cases. Their up lighting proudly cast the butt plugs, whips, gags, ropes, pommels, and various other sex toys in a soft glow. Chests lined the walls beneath the cases, which I knew held more extreme binding devices, most of them metal, which caused pain.

To our right a swing dangled from the ceiling, and a rope fitted with knots and rounded metal prongs stretched from one side of the room to the other. To our left was the bed, a dramatic four-poster, draped with every shade of black fabric imaginable. But between us stood the object of her attention: a floor to ceiling wooden X adorned with various leather cuffs and braces to bind a person to it.

My eyes returned to her; that was a mistake. Her cheeks were heated to a sexy shade of pink, chest rising and falling with each breath and her thighs– were they ever so slightly pressed together?

"Do you know what that is?" The question left my lips before I could think better of it and her gaze shot to mine.

Fuck. Those big blue eyes were fucking *begging* me. For mercy of course, not sex. Suddenly annoyed, my hand tightened on the axe, and I took another step toward her.

"What happened to all the bratty comments, Red?"

She didn't move as I closed the space between us, stepping around the X and pausing an arm's length away from her. I dropped the head of the axe on the floor, leaning my bodyweight against it to bring my face level with hers. I noted how her eyes flicked to my mask and ever so slightly heated. In response, I reached forward and gripped her chin in my fingers.

"You gonna behave?" I asked. Mistake number two.

Her eyes flashed with a bridled fury a second before she dipped her head, teeth digging into my thumb. I yanked my hand away, incredulous as I glanced between her and the bite mark on my skin.

The satisfied smirk on her face fell as she read the look in my eyes. My movements were swift as I grabbed her wrist, yanking her around to pin her between me and the X. Immediately, she began to struggle, and I hissed as she arched her ass back into me. I lifted the axe and swung.

The impact shook the X as the blade sank into the upper right arm, making the wood splinter and rain down on her head. She buried her face against the leather cushioning, shoulders rising against her neck as her body went rigid. I braced my weight on the handle of the axe, and nudged one of my knees between her legs, effectively pinning her to the spot. But then I was met with an elbow being thrown back into my ribcage.

"Enough!" I roared. My hand closed around the elbow she threw, clenching it so tight that I could feel her pulse. And that's when the first whimper tore from her throat.

I stood there perplexed for a minute. With the amount of sass she threw my way, I thought she might not have known what exactly she was getting into. That would have allowed me to drag it out, scare her, take my time. But with the way she was cowering under me, it was very clear to me now that she walked on this ship expecting her death.

My father said the women typically sought us out, promised sons or obedience, and clung to diplomacy. 'No' was never a word they'd dare utter to a Roane.

Alexandria hadn't done anything they prepared me for. Nothing about her demeanor suggested obedience was in her nature, and she sure as hell wasn't trying to be diplomatic. If anything, she marched onto this ship trying to rile me up, like she had something to prove or overcome.

Even now, as she slowly turned to look at me with tears streaming down her face, beneath the confusion and horror, there was that spark of defiance in her eyes. Is this what she was alluding to, when she baited my father about her spirit?

This was the woman I had, against my will, killed for. The one who hid herself from my family for sixteen years to try and dodge her duties. The one responsible for all my training, all my beatings. The one to blame for every monstrous act I'd been forced to commit.

And somehow, making her cry made me feel like I was the worst person alive.

12

My ass hit the floor once the door to the bathroom shut behind him.

When he had backed away, I was confused. His eyes were a vacant wall of grey, the rest of his expression hidden by the mask. They didn't meet mine again as he retrieved his axe and brushed past me, throwing a gruff 'If you weren't entertaining me, you'd be dead by now' over his shoulder before slamming the door shut behind him.

To be left relatively unscathed was a shock. My whole life, I had been prepared to meet a man that was merciless. I saw that axe and thought I was dead. And when I ended up in this room… I thought death would be lucky.

He scared me, and efficiently made his point. I nearly pissed myself when the axe impacted the St Andrews Cross, almost screamed when his knee forced my legs open. There wasn't a doubt in my mind that if I were on this ship with Jetson that would have been it for me.

But then he released me. And then he left. And my heart was still pounding in my chest like a war drum.

My legs were still shaking too hard to stand, so on my hands and knees, I dragged myself to the bathroom. I barely reached the toilet before upheaving what little I had left in my stomach.

Braxon showed no sign of returning and his voice didn't mock me from the speakers, so I didn't rush as I rinsed my mouth and washed my face. Turning to the mirror, I took in the state of my swollen eyes and matted curls. And paused.

The mirror was hanging slightly off center, the edges of the frame not meeting the rigid planes in the wall. I reached out to try and shift it back into place, and it started to fall instead. I threw myself back, afraid of being cut by shattering glass, but to my surprise the mirror wasn't falling. Gracefully, it swung open on silent hinges– it was a hidden door.

I peeked inside, staring up a cramped, winding staircase; so that's how he got down here so quickly. In either direction, a narrow corridor ran alongside the inside walls of the ship. Stepping inside, I could see the faint outline of light from the other rooms to my left and right. It was a secret passageway, with entrances only he would know about, but he was sloppy and left in such a rush that I found this entrance.

If the staircase was any indication, these corridors ran the length of each floor. I would be able to move around without setting off the motion detectors he claimed were on the main doors. Relief flooded me, as I pulled the mirror closed behind me with a soft click. Grabbing the banister, I made the dizzying climb back to C deck.

Emerging from the hidden entrance behind a locker, I nearly wept in relief seeing my bags where I dropped them. I didn't waste any more time trying to figure out which locker was which, and began to circle the room, throwing them all open. I can't completely hold back my sounds of frustration when all of them stare back at me empty.

All the doors are identical, save for the dents, so I start to study them more closely. Nothing stands out on the inside; all painted the same chipped blue. I slam the doors closed, eyes scanning their fronts for any visual differences, and my eyes snag on the one at the far end of the row.

There's two thin scratch marks in the paint, running from the top to the bottom which I hadn't noticed before. They were perfectly identical. Like an 11. With a gasp I yank my backpack to me, pulling my great grandmother's journal out and scanning the page.

C Deck. Locker 11. Remain invisible for as long as possible.

I yank the locker open again, hands running along the inside seams until my fingers brush against... nothing. I pull back confused, staring at the empty hook, before reaching forwards and grasping a silky handful of air. I blink, thinking I must be losing my mind.

I grab at the thing I can feel but can't see, carefully pulling it out of the locker. With my grip tight on the handful of nothing, I mull over Juliannas words. 'Remain invisible, for as long as possible.' If she meant it literally, then this was...

With a gasp I drop to the floor, quickly stretching out the invisible object over my legs to gauge how long it is. Then I shriek when my hand disappears. I jump, pulling my hand out of the thing and it reappears. Slowly, I repeat the process, sliding my arm deeper. Watching in a combination of horror and fascination as more and more of my body disappears before my eyes.

I jump to my feet, careful not to lose the invisible fabric as I strip down to my underwear. Rubbing my fingers along the length of it, I find a seam and– yes! I yank a teensy zipper open revealing the black inside of the invisibility suit.

I quickly inside–out the suit (complete with built–in foot covers) and eyeball it to make sure it will fit before shoving my feet in. I zip myself in, giggling at the sight of my bobbing head in the mirror. Just a few hours ago this would have been morbid, but now it's a fucking saving grace.

I reach back into the locker, carefully searching the floor and all four hooks to see if I can find a hood of some kind but come up empty handed. Glancing back at the mirror I eyed my hair– that was going to be a problem. One I could mitigate at least.

Quickly, I pull the layers back into a French braid, securing it with one of the elastics from my toiletries bag. Tucking my braid into the suit successfully hides most of the red beacon but my head is still very visible. Turning back to the locker, I open the smaller storage compartment at the top and feel around, but I come up empty handed again.

I sigh, packing my belongings into the locker before turning to look around the room again. There're some towels folded on a shelving unit near the open showers. Some sports equipment lines the otherwise empty walls. Boxes of soap and shampoo.

My eyes gravitate back to the equipment. Though this floor houses a gym, I saw nothing while I passed through that would support the play of baseball– at least I think I'm picturing the right sport. Rows of long, wooden sticks are protruding from open green duffle bags, which hold additional protective equipment like gloves and helmets.

Helmets.

I wander over to the closest bag, digging around in it for a few seconds, before my hand emerges with a helmet that's smaller than the rest and a different shape.

Growing up, my brothers would say I was too smart for my own good, or that I'd overcomplicate simple things with abstract thinking. I searched for clues more often than facts, and alternate routes rather than steady directions. That creative thinking helped me outsmart them all the time, and now it was going to keep me alive on this ship.

Turning toward the mirror, I pulled on the helmet, flicking the faceguard down and watched as my head disappeared.

13

"You never shared what you recognized in the dungeon, Red." Braxon's voice filtered lazily from the speakers above my head.

We've been drifting through space for about two weeks, and the only time we interacted was like this. Or if he decided to chase me through the ship like a psychopath with an axe to cope with his boredom and frustration.

He had gotten too close for comfort many times, the suit being the only thing that saved me. I didn't dare say a thing about it, scared he might have a way to turn it off or track it. Though it was hard to bite back all my comments. It was hilarious seeing how frustrated he got while turning in a circle, grey eyes taking quick glances down at his handheld to confirm I was still in the same room as him.

I tried not to be dumb with the rooms I stopped in. I never lingered in rooms like the gym or the pool (yes, a pool on a spaceship) which were wide open, because then he would know something was off. I also avoided the weapon room on B deck.

At first, I figured I was lucky to have his arsenal at my disposal, but the fucker locked up all his guns. There was no way I was going to get as close to him as the blades required, and I'm pretty sure if I helped myself to any of his explosives, I'd blow the whole ship up.

Instead, I stuck to rooms more advantageous for me. Of course, I favored the library. It was an intricately woven space filled with furniture and hand carved bookshelves, so it offered plenty of angles to 'stay out of sight.' Additionally, it held many interesting reads to keep me entertained. I doubt Braxon knew that there was a full collection of dirty novels on board. Shamefully, those helped me pass the time and work off some of the tension in my body.

The other room I favored, was the communications room on D deck. The space was naturally dark and stuffed to the brim with material and storage shelves, so there were plenty of explainable 'hiding spots.'

I wanted to avoid the dungeon altogether, not wanting to flirt with the idea of getting cornered in there again. But unfortunately, it also offered many good hiding spots. In desperate moments, I would use the hidden corridors and staircases (I learned there was a matching set on both sides of the ship) to go hide in there. He rarely even checked the room, probably expecting me to avoid it like the plague. Still, I wouldn't stick around once he gave up the chase for the day, retreating back to one of the rooms which were less intimidating to rest.

"I saw the look on your face." Braxon's relentless voice echoed off the kitchen's tiled floor; the speaker in here was more powerful than the others onboard. I could practically hear the smirk in his voice as he added, "You were flushed. You saw something in there you liked. What was it?" I sighed and yanked open the refrigerator door.

"The St Andrews Cross. That's what I recognized," I responded, purposefully emphasizing the last word.

There had been a rough sketch of one in the third Thorne diary, and though the colors didn't match, it was undoubtedly the same contraption. I shivered inadvertently, unable to imagine how any of the descriptions of its use could be pleasant with a Roane in the room.

"What's that?" He asked. I blinked, staring up at the speaker but he stayed silent.

"You expect me to believe you don't know what it is? Nice try." I tried not to let his words knock me off guard, and continued to make myself a quick meal.

Though I never saw a servant, most of the food here was already prepped, so I just had to heat it up. If I had to actually cook for myself, I'd starve to death within a week.

"Sorry, Red, I didn't exactly have a lot of time to fuck at military school." The frankness of his comment nearly made me drop the plate I was holding.

"R–right," I stammered, turning on the oven and setting the plate on the counter while it preheated.

"So, are you gonna explain it to me or leave me wondering?" He chuckled, and I fought the urge to laugh along with him.

Come on, it *was* a ridiculous notion. Me, the pristine debutant, recognizing such an extreme, sexual device. Still, I refrain from entertaining him, and will my voice to sound bored in my reply.

"Why the hell would I do that?"

"I still can't get over how colorful your vocabulary is," he chuckled again, "I genuinely have never heard a lady curse."

"Never been much of a lady," I muttered and crossed my arms. I didn't flinch as the kitchen door swung open, growing accustomed to his random appearances.

He always looked the same. Black jacket, black pants, black boots, and of course that stupid black mask. He'd refrained from going barefoot after day two when I had broken a glass and sprinkled the shards just inside the kitchen door where he now stood.

I learned that that's where he started hunting me most times, as he sealed himself in the captain's office just across the main deck. That axe of his hung loosely from his hand, the tip resting against the tile as his grey eyes scanned the room.

"Did you have a tutor who specialized in the subject of hiding?" He muttered, stepping to the left towards one of the pantries.

I held my breath not taking the bait. The first and only time I had responded, his axe had swung for my head (technically the door behind my head but he couldn't see me), so I tiptoed to the right towards another hidden servant's entrance.

My initial thought had been correct—the servants' doors didn't trigger the device in his hands. In total, there were ten of them on each deck, one on each side of every room. I rarely used the main doors now, just often enough to keep him in the dark about what I'd learned, and I never bothered with the elevator. Watching him get doubly pissed off when he couldn't find me *and* didn't know where I was, was both hilarious and nerve wracking.

In a sick way, it was simply thrilling. Not the threats of murder or the axe-swinging part, but the outsmarting him part. And the chase; that alone woke up some forgotten, primal part of me which never before existed. Already, I could feel the adrenaline pumping in my veins, anticipation on my tongue as I neared the hidden latch to the servant corridor: a light switch that was actually a door handle in the wall.

I flicked it and he turned at the noise. My fingers hovered on the panel, wanting to push in and disappear down the corridor, but there would be no way to explain a hole opening in the wall by itself, so I restrained myself.

Slowly, he rounded the island. But then the oven dinged, signaling that it was time to put my dinner in. He paused, and the second he glanced down at my discarded plate I was gone, the door slamming shut behind me.

There was a muffled curse and a bang, most likely my plate being thrown against the wall after me. I bolted into a sprint for the spiral staircase which would lead me down and away.

The first time I was chased in here, I didn't dare turn around until reaching the stairs. To my surprise, he was already ducking into the room directly next to the one I fled from. I had forgotten I was invisible, so he couldn't see me standing there in the center of the aisle about to scream.

I've been pulling the same maneuver ever since, duck in the servant's corridor, run to the stairs, or the opposite end, and wait for him to exit first. I suppressed a giggle as the door slammed open behind me, dropping onto the first step and leaning against the railing to watch him as he decided which door to exit.

But he wasn't sprinting after me today. No, he was stalking the corridor. His grey eyes scanned every inch of the space before him, his boots echoing dull thuds with each slow step.

"I don't know how you're doing it, but I know you're hiding in here." His voice came out in a twisted snarl and I recoiled. This was not good. He lifted the axe, bringing it down to crack open the floor.

"Is there some hidden corner in here I don't know about?" He yelled, swinging the axe again, this time into the wall. It tore a gash through the sheet metal, but he continued to hit it repeatedly, as if he was possessed.

Sparks began spraying from ripped wires as he worked his way down the corridor. I back pedaled down the first few steps, a yelp slipping past my lips as an alarm sounded and steam hissed through one of the tears he left in the wall. His eyes locked on the stairs; head cocked like a predator.

He took a single step towards me. Automatically I took another step back, the soles of the suit squeaking against the metal step. Slowly, he slid his hand into his pocket for the handheld we both knew hadn't gone off while he raged. When he spoke, his statement might as well have been the only sound in the small space.

"You found the suit, didn't you?"

My jaw dropped open under the helmet, unable to utter a single thing as he approached the top of the stairs. With just four steps between us, I could now see how haggard he looked.

Dark circles made his eyes appear sunken in. His hair was tangled, and probably unwashed. I couldn't help but feel a misplaced appreciation as he raised the hem of his T-shirt to wipe the sweat from his forehead. But this close to his bare skin, I noticed something new.

He was packed with muscle, and seemed untouchable, so the brief glimpse of the scars littering his torso took me off guard. A bitter taste filled my mouth as his words about military school echoed in my head, and despite everything, I felt myself worrying about him. The hidden scars and clear exhaustion reminded me of the times Colby returned from a few of his harsher training sessions.

Braxon's eyes were gazing straight through me, past me down the winding stairs, searching. As if he was lonely and wanted my company.

But then he jerked back, his axe swinging up to rest on his shoulder as he walked away from me back towards the captain's office, saying over his shoulder, "I hope you're having fun."

The door swung shut behind him and a few moments later the alarm overhead stopped blaring. Cowering in that stairwell, I had never been more confused in my life.

14

I had been dreading this moment, but I couldn't put it off any longer: I needed to shower. It's officially been 18 days since boarding *The Ladyship* and I reeked. My braid was greasy, and all my panties were dirty. I had opted to only wear those under the suit with a tank, as chafing became problematic with too many layers. And sweating.

At the very least, all my clothes were dry and clean, so I would have something to cover myself with while I waited for the suit to dry. It was the first thing I planned to wash, preferring to have that clean over myself if in case Ax decided to come after me halfway through my shower.

It made me slightly uncomfortable that I had given him a nickname, even if it was just in my head. But considering 'Ax' was literally IN his name, and he chased me with one, well, it was unavoidable.

I hid myself in the library until the lights dimmed at 14 solar hours, then waited for hopefully another 2 before creeping downstairs into the locker room.

In the dull glow of the nightlights which lined the floor, I located the boxes stacked against the wall. I'd discovered one held bar soap and detergent, and retrieved some to quickly wash. Then I opened the locker I stored my bags in, and was surprised to find my beauty products were still there. Well, most of them at least. My shampoo and conditioner were accounted for, but my leave–in detangler was nowhere to be found. I gritted my teeth, knowing Ax had probably swiped it in retaliation.

Obviously, he knew I had the suit (making me wonder how he knew of the suit and why it was left on the ship in the first place) but seriously what did he expect of me?

To not wear it and sit around waiting to be murdered?

Ugh, the suit. I peeled it off me, the sweaty fabric clinging to my legs. Inside–outing it, I laid it on the tiled floor under one of the showerheads, turning the water to warm and let it pour down on it for a good five minutes before scrubbing the detergent into it. There was a washer and dryer in one of the rooms downstairs, but I was afraid of the noise drawing his attention.

Next, I moved onto my panties, washing all of them quickly and hanging them to dry in the first stall. After ringing out the suit. I rinsed myself off, tugging my hair from the braid and massaging my scalp.

As I worked the shampoo into my curls, I felt my muscles relaxing for the first time in weeks, a sudden soreness roaring from many places at once. I had slept once a day, but fitfully and only for a few hours. I never stayed in one room for long, trying to

strategically avoid Ax, or moving out of sheer
boredom. I'd camped out in corners, squatted
in crevices, and had been running
everywhere.

I sat on the floor next to the suit,
massaging in between my sore toes, and
gently rubbing the new callouses on my
abused feet. I avoided thinking about how
much longer I could keep this up while
reaching for the conditioner.

Once everything was rinsed, I lifted
one of the sleeping shirts Jules had added to
my duffle bag, and pulled it over my head.
The plain black shirt was cashmere, and long
enough to brush my thighs. I hoped it would
be enough to hide me in the dark if he
decided to seek me out.

Then I reached for the suit, flipping it
back to the invisible side, and hung it inside
the last stall to dry. It might take an extra
minute to get it, especially if it fell, but at
least Ax wouldn't find it.

I didn't know how to clean the helmet without destroying it, so I just dampened a washcloth and rubbed around inside for a few minutes. I decided to place it in the equipment bag I'd found it in to dry.

Then I got to work on my curls. It was hell. Even after letting the conditioner process, I couldn't even get my fingers to drag through, let alone a brush. I groaned out in frustration, resisting the urge to chuck the brush at the mirror.

If I were Ax, where would I hide the detangler? A strained laugh bubbled out of me as I paced, contemplating, before a full on doubled-over giggle fit took me over. This was completely nuts.

Here I was, stuck on a floating ship in space, my only companion a homicidal maniac, and I was trying to figure out where he hid my detangler. It was enough to bring tears to my eyes. That at least finally grounded me, and I quickly blinked back the burning sensation, refusing to let any of them drop. I would not cry for him again.

Before I could think better of it, I slipped on a pair of shoes and grabbed my grandfather's pocketknife. Quietly, I swung the mirror open and began climbing the circular staircase up to A deck. I made my way to the captain's office, hesitating when my fingers closed around the door's handle. The shade on the window was drawn, and no noise echoed from within, so I took a breath and flung the door open.

The space was immaculate. A long table ran down the center of the room, covered with glowing buttons, some blinking, and various switches. A machine against the back wall was whirring softly, the surface covered with dials measuring different pressures with red needles. It took me a minute to spot Ax, draped in a chair at the far end of the room. And curse me, I think I started drooling.

He was asleep, shirtless. The amount of muscle in his body should be considered a crime. Again, I got the urge to touch him, wondering if his skin would feel soft or rough. Mentally, I smacked myself, settling on counting the scars crisscrossing his abdomen and chest.

There were so many, standing pale against his otherwise bronze skin, and for the second time I felt myself getting rattled on his behalf. Just what the hell did they do to him? I dragged my gaze up to his face. His dark hair was flung over the back of the chair, but to my disappointment, that damn mask was still on.

Silently, I tiptoed across the room trying to figure out the best approach to the situation. I doubted he would remain asleep if I started digging through the cabinets in the room. Likewise, waking him up at knifepoint and demanding he reveal where my detangler was seemed equally pathetic. But as fate would have it, my decision was made for me.

Just as I reached the end of the table in front of him, Ax's eyes flew open. He wasn't delirious or confused. He didn't bolt out of his seat in shock or rage. With a sinking feeling, I realized he hadn't been asleep at all.

15

A month ago, if you had told me that I would wake up in my office with my wife straddling my lap in the middle of the night, I might have laughed. But here I was, yanking her towards me so she didn't bolt.

I caught her easily, trapping her against my chest as she tumbled into the chair on top of me. I was delirious when she walked in, enough so that I laid still, curious to see what she would do. But now the panic in her eyes woke me fully and was the only thing which kept me from making a stupid comment. That and the cold touch of a blade to my throat.

I had no idea where she got the knife. The blade felt too small to be from my stash downstairs, maybe it was a fancy kind of peeling knife from the kitchen? I doubted it. I watched this woman try to cook and it was pathetic. By day three, she opted for just stealing the food I had prepared for myself.

At first that pissed me off, but lately I found it kinda… adorable. Hearing her triumphant little squeaks through the comm in my ear, followed by the quick steps of her running from the kitchen after warming the plate, pleased something in me.

For a while, I fought against that mounting presence, but the longer we were here the more demanding it became. And the quieter my rage seemed to get.

I soon found myself getting creative with what I made. Not because I was trying to impress her, but her dying of starvation wasn't exactly on my to-do list. And it definitely wouldn't satisfy the brutal fantasies my father envisioned for her. Not that she would know that.

"You took my detangler." Her voice cut through my thoughts, bringing me back to the moment at hand.

Alexandria had braced a knee on the arm of the chair, putting some distance between us. That did nothing to erase the memory of her ass pressed against my cock just moments before. I swallowed; my voice perfectly flat when I replied.

"I did." Her blue eyes flashed, annoyed. I snorted under the mask. It was too easy to pull a reaction from her, and she didn't even know it.

"I need it," she hissed, frowning.

"You don't say?" My hand, which had been playing with the ends of her damp hair, now drifted down to trace the curve of her hip through the nightshirt. She tensed under my touch, not enough to move, but enough for me to feel. Slowly, I grinned.

So, I wasn't the only one with inappropriately mixed feelings. If that were the case, I wanted to see how far she would let me push.

"Where is it?" She demanded, ignoring my wandering hands.

"Now if I answer that, you'll leave." I leaned forward a bit, wanting to catch a whiff of her. Shockingly, she eased the knife back instead of slicing into me, so I went ahead and inhaled against her neck. Eucalyptus and rose; the scent made my head spin.

"I'll leave anyway," she muttered, moving to fully stand. Out of my control, my hand wound around the end of her wet hair again, yanking her back down against me.

I groaned at the contact. Her nipples were peaked through her shirt, the nubs pressing into my bare chest. Her legs clenched around mine, as if trying to lift her sex (which I'm fairly certain was bare) away from me. Surprise coursed through me as I realized I was tempted to remove my mask so that I could get a proper taste of her skin. I felt her shiver against me, and the blade at my throat wobbled ever so slightly.

"I'm not gonna give you your detangler," I said, ignoring the plea in her eyes. I dropped her hair, leaning back in my seat, "I'll bring it to you when you shower so you can use it, but you'll have to tell me when that is instead of sneaking around in the dark."

Her jaw dropped and I reached out, rubbing my thumb against her bottom lip. She jerked back as if I'd electrocuted her.

"Never mind then!" She forcefully pushed off me this time, muttering, "I guess I'll just shave my head."

A low growl rumbled in my chest. Before I realized what I was doing, I was on my feet, scooping her in my arms. Her knife clattered to the floor as I dumped her ass on my desk.

With one hand firmly pressing down against her thigh, I knelt, picking it up to examine the blade. Damn, it was sharp, small

but sharp. I flipped it closed, sliding it into
the back pocket of my jeans.

A whine pulled from her throat,
dragging my attention back to her. The pain
in her eyes confused me before I realized my
hand had drifted higher, now drilling against
her sternum and keeping her pinned to the
wall. I yanked it back, and both of us blinked
in surprise.

"Stay there," I muttered, turning
before she could say anything, and started
rifling through the drawers next to us.

She visibly relaxed when I held up the
bottle of detangler, and was bold enough to
slowly reach out for it. Automatically I
grabbed her wrist, earning myself another
annoyed glare. I beat back my own confused
thoughts, chalking it up to being overtired as
I heard myself say, "Nope. Tell me how to do
it."

"What do you mean?"

Instead of replying, I dropped her hand and pumped some of the liquid into my palm. Her eyes widened as she realized what I meant to do. I stood there, hands sticky with the product as she debated for a few minutes, finally yielding with a small nod.

"Start at the ends and work your way up to the roots."

"Okay."

"You're gonna need more product than that."

"Okay."

"It's my only bottle. I'll need another–"

"Will you just shut up?" I hissed, threading my fingers into her hair.

I worked in silence, occasionally prodding her to check if I needed to add more of the product to my hands. When we got to the point of my fingers massaging into her scalp, her eyes drifted shut, and I knew I was lingering much longer than necessary.

Initially, I stole it because it looked fancy and unnecessary, but I could see the difference now. When she arrived, her curls were coarse to the touch and dull. Even though her hair wasn't yet dry, it had smoothed, and gained that fiery shine. Forcing myself to stop touching her, I dropped the bottle back into the drawer before she could protest.

"Seriously?" She arched a brow, "What do you gain from holding that hostage?" Well, that was an interesting choice of words, but I didn't back down.

"If I'm lucky, I'll get to see you naked." A blush coated her cheeks, but I added, "Though I'll settle for knowing you're taking care of yourself."

"Why does that matter?" Something in her tone shifted, the wariness returning to her eyes. I mentally kicked myself.

"Look," I fumbled for a believable excuse, "I'm not gonna kill you while you're in the shower. That goes for sleeping and eating as well. The way I see it, is if you outsmart me, it's not my right to cheat and take you out in a vulnerable state like that."

"Cheat?" She snorted and I gawked at her, but she ignored me as she said, "You're talking about this as if it's a game."

"Isn't it?" I lowered my voice, edging closer so that I was standing fully between her legs. Her throat bobbed, eyes flicking down to my bare chest before back up to my face. I pinned her with my stare, annoyance creeping in that she had gotten this far under my skin. Making her feel a bit of shame would be an appropriate punishment. I brushed her hair to the side, leaning in.

"Even though I can't see you with that suit on, I can damn near taste your excitement. Your adrenaline. Even now, your body is practically begging me to chase you."

Her lips parted in shock, breaths picking up. Satisfaction spread through me as

I watched her search for a denial she didn't have. Ever so slowly, I slid my hand under the hem of her shirt, fingers grazing the inside of her thigh. She snapped her jaw shut, hands finding purchase on my shoulders and shoved. I barely moved.

"Are you fighting me, or yourself?" I whispered, dragging my fingers from the top of her thigh to rise over the swell of her hip, "Because you're not wearing any panties."

"They were dirty!" She hissed, digging her nails into my skin. "They're drying, along with the suit."

"Ah, so that's why I can see you." She froze as my hand dove between her legs, hovering just above her heat. I snickered, "And is it safe to assume you shaved?"

"My mother made me wax!" She groaned, leaning her head back against the wall as my index finger parted her folds. She. Was. Soaked.

"Mhm," I didn't think about what I was doing, just started working her clit in slow circles, increasing the pressure each time around. "I don't think your mother trained you how to get this wet, though I'm certainly not complaining."

She sucked in a breath as I replaced my finger with my thumb, sliding the former into her without hesitation.

"S–stop..." she whispered through clenched teeth.

"Why should I? Did you forget you belong to me now, Red?" I watched her begin to squirm as I pumped the digit in and out in rhythm with my circling thumb. My cock strained against my zipper, but I ignored it.

Internally, I was at war with myself. The vicious half of me wanted to break her down till there was nothing left but a shell to kill. But my intrigue was growing into something ravenous, and it was getting drunk on the sounds she was letting slip loose.

A strangled noise tore from her throat as I slid a second finger into her, and my free hand rose to curl around her neck. There was a shift in her demeanor then, so subtle that anyone else most likely would have missed it. But trained as I was, it was impossible to ignore.

Her grip on my arms was no longer resistant, her fingers curling against my skin now rather than pushing away. And her hips were lifting ever so slightly each time my fingers curled in. She wasn't simply taking it because I was making her: she was taking it because she wanted it.

"That's it," I murmured, "ride my fingers till you come apart, Red."

Moments later she shuddered, and I felt her walls clamp around me. I pressed my thumb flat to her clit, slowing my movements as her breath evened out, before dropping my hold on her altogether.

I could feel her eyes on me as I crossed the room, finding a towel to wipe my hand on. Something in me howled about not licking my fingers clean but I ignored it.

"I–is that it?" She asked, and this time I did laugh out loud.

"Oh, you *want* me to touch you? Sorry, with all the running the past few weeks, I've kinda gotten mixed signals."

She bristled as I crossed the room towards her, but I just dropped back into my chair, assuming the same position as when she entered. I arched a brow at her when she didn't move.

"Are you gonna sit there and watch me sleep, Red?"

Her cheeks turned that very color as she finally slid from the desk and left the room. I laughed again, stretching my arms

over my head before settling back. As I
drifted off, my brain decided it was the
perfect moment to point out I hadn't once
tried to hurt her like I was supposed to.

16

I'm officially mentally ill.

Sleep did not find me, instead my brain decided to replay the interaction over and over. It seemed hyper fixed on the fact that his skin smelled like leather and sweat, that his fingers in my hair sent my stomach flip flopping, that when I climaxed his grey eyes went wholly black.

I kept enough of my pride to walk from the room, but broke into a full sprint as soon as the door shut behind me. I cleaned myself up in less than a minute, not caring that my panties and suit were still damp when I tugged them on. The only silver lining was that when his back was turned, I swiped a set of extra comms he left on the desk next to me.

I spent the remainder of the night fiddling with the suit's helmet, half terrified that I would break it. I had never been more grateful for Samuel's insistence that I join some of my brothers more advanced engineering lectures, than when a small pop of static echoed simultaneously from inside the helmet and the speaker above.

The lights turned back on about an hour ago, and the white tile of the locker room momentarily blinded me. I stuffed my things back into my locker and slammed it shut, creeping into the servant's corridor and went to the library. Only then did I raise the helmet over my head and turn it into place.

"Can you hear me?" I asked, hearing my voice echo slightly from the speaker in the room.

"Clear as day." Ax's voice in my ear immediately made me shiver, but he didn't sound upset. If anything, he sounded pleased. "I didn't pin you for a thief, but here you are, stealing another thing that belongs to me."

"Considering you stole from me first, we're even," I muttered, kicking open the main door of the library. I propped it open behind me, before settling into the window seat to wait.

"Ah, but did I steal first?" I heard his chair scrape the floor, and made a mental note that the comms were more sensitive than the main speakers.

"Don't tell me you forgot about last night?" I hissed and immediately regretted my words. "The hair detangler," I quickly clarified, "you took something I need, so I took something too." My cheeks burned as I heard him chuckle.

"And here I thought you were referring to something else. But, you do realize I didn't steal from you first?" At my silence he added, "Just where do you think all those prepped meals are coming from Red? Have you seen any servants on this ship?" I gasped, realization dawning on me.

"Have I been stealing your food?"

"For the first three days, yes." He snorted, "From then on I just made double so that *I* didn't starve."

I was floored. We've been on this ship for weeks, which means throughout our cohabitation he's been cooking for me at least twice a day. And didn't poison me once.

"Thank you," I said awkwardly as he appeared in the library door. He was in his usual full black, and his axe was propped on his shoulder. I tried not to look at it as I whispered, "But I'm afraid I'm going to piss you off again."

"You do that daily." His eyes scanned the room, "but do enlighten me."

"I wired your spare comm to my helmet, essentially making me invisible and soundproof." His axe slipped a few inches, and I stifled a laugh.

"Where the hell did you learn how to do that?"

"I took a few classes with my brothers," I mused, lifting my feet from the floor to sit cross legged.

"So, she's beautiful and intelligent." There was no judgement in his tone, but I bristled anyway.

"Don't call me that." He shrugged,

"Fine, you're a dumb bitch. Better?" Sarcasm laced every word as he ran a hand through his hair. As it was, it constantly hung in his face, hiding what little I could see. It aggravated me that he didn't tie it back, and my awareness of that aggravated me further.

"Seems more appropriate a comment from someone who wants to kill me." His eyes flicked straight toward me while I spoke that time, but they quickly passed over, scanning the dark crevices between the bookshelves.

"I want to break you. Not kill you. There's a difference." His voice was rough, stifling an emotion I couldn't place.

"Sorry, with all the axe swinging the past few weeks I've gotten mixed signals." The mocking words flew from my mouth before I could think better of it and he stiffened, looking up at the weapon as if he just realized he had it.

"You really know how to work me up don't you?" He muttered, twirling the axe once before slamming it full force into the side of the closest bookshelf. He dusted his hands off.

"I'd clap for that bravado, but I don't wanna give myself away." I didn't bother trying to mask the laughter in my voice. He arched a brow as he slid his gaze back to me.

"Even though I know you're seated at the window?"

I felt a rock drop in my stomach. Immediately, I slid my feet to the floor, but he was faster. The seat was built for two, but small enough for him to find me rather easily.

He caged me in between his arms, hunching over to press his palms flat against the glass at my back. His voice was laced with a mocking triumph as he whispered, "I might not be able to see you, but your shadow shows up just as good."

I mentally kicked myself. There I was, shooting my mouth off with my back to a window full of STARS. I might as well have stripped off the suit and waved when he came in.

One of his arms dropped to wrap around my waist, pulling me to the edge of the seat. Then he dropped a knee to the floor, forcing my legs open so he could rest between them. His hands slowly traced up my front, coming to a halt at my neck. I heard the latch of the helmet click open as he said, "How about we get you out of this thing and finish what you started last night?"

Panic took over and in one swift move I pulled my head back– before slamming the helmet into his face as hard as I could.

She broke my fucking nose.

My ass hit the floor, and I didn't even try to stop it. Black edged my vision, and my hands flew up to my face as I felt the blood start to gush.

I don't know if she stayed or ran but at this point, I didn't care. My fingers shook as I reached behind my head, yanking my hair as I undid the buckle holding the mask to my face. I let it fall to the floor, a torrent of blood following it.

I heard her gasp through the speakers and footsteps approaching behind me, but I threw out a hand, "Don't fucking look at me." I tried to sound scary, but the pain was working against me.

"I didn't mean to–"

"Wherever the fuck you are just stay there." The command came through gritted teeth as I tilted my head back and positioned my thumbs. With a snap I set my nose, a fresh stream of blood rushing from it.

Then I felt a hand on my shoulder and stiffened, glancing down to actually *see* her shaking fingers gripping the lapel of my jacket. One bare arm was visible, and the screen on her helmet was lifted, revealing her face. I kept my hands over my nose, afraid that if I moved a muscle she would bolt.

"Will you let me help you?" The unconcealed concern in her gaze made the corners of her eyes glitter.

Fifteen minutes later we were in my office again– me slouched in my chair and her hovering over me checking the gauze we stuffed into my nose. The bleeding had stopped a while ago, but I didn't say a word.

When we first arrived, my nose started bleeding again for a whole other reason: she was naked under that suit! She didn't waste any time scooping a pair of my sweatpants and a shirt off the floor and snapping at me to close my eyes.

Blaming it on the blood loss, I did as she said, turning my chair around for good measure. I think I even gave myself a splinter from gripping the arms of the chair so hard to resist the urge to grab that long braid of hers.

With a damp cloth, she dabbed at the dried blood, cleaning off my nose and my mouth. The wounded cartilage screamed against the contact, but I remained still, watching her. She hadn't offered an explanation, or made a single comment about my face, so I just focused on the icepack she settled on the bridge of my nose and willed it to numb me faster.

I must have dozed off, because when I next sat up, she was gone. On the table next to me was a plate filled with overboiled spaghetti noodles and a card. I smirked as I picked it up, eyes roving over the elegant handwriting inside.

'I never thought of myself as a violent person until I came on this ship. You'll be pleased to know that you have terrified me on more than one occasion, but most often you confuse me.

I was raised to expect a painful, merciless death from you. That's not an excuse for my own behaviors, but I believe it a fair explanation.

Also, I washed your mask while you slept. There was quite a bit of blood in it. I left it hanging in the kitchen to dry.

~Alexandria'

I dropped the card back on the desk, before lowering my head into my hands. It was an apology. Nothing mocking. No questions. That, paired with the consideration I did nothing to deserve, was like a knife through my gut.

I should have killed her weeks ago, but I've hesitated. And now, I wasn't sure I wanted to.

Before my thoughts could spiral any further, one of the monitors behind me blinked to life with the gentle chime of a new message. I sat up, glancing at the screen and bile instantly rose in my throat. My family letterhead glared back at me. I've ignored too many messages to not read this one. With a heavy breath, I opened it, eyes scanning the text warily.

'Braxon,

I expected this matter to be promptly dealt with. If your childlike behaviors persist, I will be forced to intervene as your skills are necessary elsewhere.

Send that woman's head home on a spike or you'll find the food will stop coming.'

My fist flew into the screen, glass shattering my father's threat before my eyes.

18

I went back to the library to clean up the blood, before retreating to the locker room. His blood had stained both the helmet and the suit, so I had to wash it again. Then with nothing to do, I went upstairs to the planetarium, and just stared out into the vast endlessness.

What the hell happened to him? I refused to acknowledge that it wasn't my business, or that I shouldn't develop any sort of care for him considering his rampages. But after seeing that jagged scar on his face, I suddenly had a new perspective on our situation.

The Roanes find pride in their volatile reputation, each generation striving to make the next even more ruthless than the last. But I never imagined the lengths they would go to guarantee it. Also, I never imagined that some of them might not wish to be that way, but had to conform to survive.

I was pacing the room now, his sweatpants tripping me every few feet. On one of these stumbles, I had to catch myself against one of the many interactive tables in the room.

The screen lit up as my hand accidentally slapped a few buttons, the sudden swirling colors projecting in the otherwise black room making me yelp. I heard a snort behind me and whipped around, finding Ax leaning in the doorway watching me from beneath his mask.

I feigned interest in the video playing on the screen, a history of when we first discovered space. Our home solar system, The Milky Way, swirled to life in front of me. I felt him at my back a few moments later, his hand sliding to turn the screen off.

"Are you going to say anything or just be a creep?" I asked, voice soft.

"I don't know, I'm pretty good at being a creep." I felt a slight tug on my braid, like a request for me to turn around. I didn't budge and he sighed, "Alexandria."

I glanced over my shoulder. Although his voice was demanding, his eyes were soft. I reached up brushing a lock of that persistent hair of his off his forehead and his brows shot upwards before he grabbed my wrist. I frowned.

"So, you can finger me, but I can't touch your face?"

"It might not come as a surprise that I don't like my face being touched." He was practically snarling, but I didn't flinch.

"You don't scare me." That was the wrong thing to say.

I was shoved backwards, splayed out on top of the screen, and he pounced on top of me. We struggled for a minute before his hands got a grip on my arms, pinning them. I started kicking, but he expertly tangled his legs with mine. Then his eyes darkened, and he thrust his hips forward, making me freeze.

Despite the layers between us, the hard column of his erection sent my nerves dancing. And if I continued to struggle like this, I'd practically be grinding myself against him.

"Are you done with your fit?"

"Are you *kidding* me–"

"I'm not kidding at all, Red." I clamped my lips shut, chest heaving with the effort to breathe under his weight.

He shifted slightly, one hand adamantly squeezing my wrists together and the other reaching into his back pocket. My grandfather's pocketknife flashed in front of my face.

"Do you know what this is?" He asked, resting the blade against my cheek.

"M–my grandfathers–"

"Yes." He cut me off, the blade skimming my skin ever so softly as he dragged it over my jawline, "It definitely is your grandfather's pocketknife. But, do you know who your grandfather was married to?" I shivered as he leaned into my neck, as if he were breathing me in.

"The answer is, Julianna." His voice was muffled between the mask and my neck, but there was no chance I misheard him as he added, "You have her diary, I believe."

"N–no." I stammered, very aware of the blade now shredding the thin material of my shirt– *his* shirt. I began to stutter an explanation, "Julianna was my great grandmother. A whole generation before."

"No," He countered, "she was married to your grandfather, Sebastian Roane. Says so right here." He tapped the hilt against my chin before holding the blade level with my eyes.

In curving text against the metal, the word *'Sebastian'* was printed. Ax flipped it to show the opposite side which read, *'Julie'.*

I cursed under my breath. It was a stolen blade, and I never had the need to open it before, so I had no clue. Ax continued, disregarding the confused screaming in my brain.

"The eldest Thorne daughter had died shortly before she was supposed to be gifted. As the second daughter, Julianna was the best available option for him. It was a match that wasn't supposed to happen, as she was half his age and couldn't bear children. Luckily, Sebastian had plenty of bastards to carry on his legacy, and a soft spot for her wit."

I gasped as the flat of the blade pressed against my now exposed nipple, unable to keep my hips from bucking against him. Ax didn't bother stifling his pleased groan as his erection rubbed against me in sweet promise.

I felt so stupid. An hour ago, I was coddling him. Less than five minutes ago I felt bad for him. And now he was… I wasn't even sure. Threatening me? No, this felt more like banter. And it shouldn't.

"Furthermore" he continued oblivious to my internal spiral, "I think you'll be interested to know that suit of yours was something she brought onto this ship. She had no intention of giving herself over meekly, and must have left it in hopes to protect her descendants. For obvious reasons, my father and I could never find it," his eyes glittered, baiting me, "but I'm not wholly bothered by that now."

"I'm not interested in anything you have to say!" I hissed, beginning to squirm under him again. Truthfully, my brain was spinning with the information about my great grandmother.

It made sense. Her diary was the only one which ever mentioned the location of the suit, and was obscure enough for no one to understand unless they went searching for it.

"Well would you rather I shut up and fuck you instead?" His words hit me like a blow, knocking me flat back against the table. He sighed, sitting up but kept my legs pinned under him. There was a click and the mask dropped from his face.

"I'm so confused," I breathed out.

It was impossible not to see the scar, a jagged white half–moon connecting the corner of his lips up to his right ear. It was as if someone held his mouth open and sawed across his face. As if they were trying to make him ugly, but failed.

The grey of his eyes just made his rosy lips more pronounced. His nose was swollen and bruised from my earlier hit, but I could tell the angle complimented his high cheekbones and impressive jawline. My fingers reached up of their own accord, tracing the 5 o'clock shadow of stubble which darkened the natural angles of his face.

"You're telling me." His voice was so low it took me a minute to realize he even replied.

Finding my courage I gripped his legs, using him as leverage to sit up. I did my best to ignore the cold passage of air over my exposed breasts, and slowly rubbed my thumb against his bottom lip as he had done to me. He literally bared his teeth when I neared the corner of his mouth.

"Oh please, I'm not going to purposefully touch it." My eyes flash back to his in annoyance, but don't edge my touch any farther.

I take a breath, checking my temper. We were on the precipice of something here, and one shove would send us over the edge into an oblivion I was unsure if I feared or craved. I softened my voice into a whisper,

"You don't need to cover it on my account. It's okay."

The snarl on his face disintegrated into a wounded look of shock, the steel wall of his eyes cracking enough for me to see past the intimidating façade he wore. And what I saw was pain, so much pain that the breath rushed out of me.

I went to pull my hand away, but one of his darted out like a laser to snatch my wrist midair. Then the other came up between us and closed around my throat. His grip was loose enough for me to still breathe, but tight enough to make my pulse begin to race.

"A–ax wait!" The words tumbled out of me, my free hand pressing against his chest desperately, "I won't touch you again, I'm sorry!"

I braced myself, eyes squeezing shut against his near–black gaze and prepared for the pain he'd been promising to deliver since

I met him. Instead, he did something I never could have prepared for: he kissed me.

She let out a yelp, but I ignored it. I was busy trying to silence the hell inside my head, and her mouth did just the trick. My hands swept the ruined shirt right off her, before greedily snaking up her sides to fondle her breasts.

"Open your mouth," I demanded, not giving her time to question me before sliding my tongue in.

I pushed her back down against the projection table, easing her into a slow, lewd kiss that had her nipples puckering under my palms. *Fuck* she was responsive.

She released a whine, both fists coming down against my shoulders. I've had just about enough of that. I angled my head, sinking my teeth into the juncture of her neck and shoulder and she gasped, stilling. I continued to explore her skin; mouth drifting even lower to trace the shape of her collarbone. Before I lost all sense and sucked one of her nipples into my mouth I jerked back, releasing my hold on her.

"You have about thirty seconds to leave this room. I'm not stopping if you stay." She just stared at me, seconds ticking by in silence. "Come on," I urged, my voice strained, "you literally were punching me a few seconds ago."

"I–I couldn't breathe." She whispered, cheeks flushing with embarrassment. I felt my eyes bugging out of my head and she dropped my gaze, "That's all...I just couldn't breathe."

"Five seconds." I ground out. Her eyes snapped back to mine, shining with a silent dare.

"Four," she whispered, and I gaped at her. She cocked a brow, "What? I thought you were good at being a creep?" A rush of air left my nose as I yanked her off the table, forcing her to her knees on the floor.

"Times up. Keep that smart mouth of yours wide open." I never needed my belt undone faster, my aching cock nearly springing from my pants before her.

Her lips were set in a thin line, fear etching her features, but there was curiosity too. I landed a light smack to her cheek, "I said open your mouth, Red." She hesitated but did as I said. Satisfaction spread through me.

"Relax your throat," I instructed, stifling a groan as I pumped a third of my length into her waiting mouth. Her breasts swayed as we moved, almost making me lose my shit right there.

Gritting my teeth I reached around the back of her head, grabbing her braid. I tugged it experimentally and she jerked forward, half my cock disappearing between her lips.

"Perfect," I growled as she eased back. I yanked her hair a bit harder this time so she would take me deeper. On her own, she lifted her tongue to drag the underside of my shaft, flicking slightly at the head. I hissed, ramming myself back into her mouth and her hands flew up to brace herself against my thighs, but that was it: she'd found her rhythm.

I kept ahold of her braid even though she didn't need me to tug her forward anymore to take my cock. For such a sheltered girl, she was sucking me off like I was her last god damn meal.

Before I wound up spilling into her mouth, I pulled all the way out. She fought me slightly, lips releasing me with a pop. Immediately, I pulled her to her feet, spinning her around so her elbows were braced on the table.

"Spread your legs," I said, yanking my shirt over my head.

"B–but–"

"I gave you your chance to run, but you decided to enjoy sucking my cock." My fingers easily slid under the waistband of the sweats and her panties, yanking them both down to her ankles. She shivered once, before stepping out of the discarded clothes.

"I've never done this," she mumbled, but stayed bent over the table. "I was told it hurts."

"At first," I confirmed, voice grating as I added, "I don't know how to convince you I'm not making it hurt on purpose."

All this talking was driving me mad. Unable to contain myself, I reached under her, spreading her sex open with my index and forefinger. She tried to pull away, but I yanked her hips back towards me, "Don't ever try to fucking hide yourself from me. You're mine, Alexandria."

She tensed when the head of my cock nudged at her entrance, sinking in those first few delicious inches. I was going slow, some delusional part of my brain acknowledging the irrefutable fact that seeing her in pain disgusted me.

Inch by inch I slid in, then out, doing my best to allow her body to adjust. By the third thrust, I was deep enough to hit resistance, so I leaned over her and pressed my palm to her mouth.

"Bite through the pain. Don't stop until it stops." And with that, I snapped that thin strip of flesh and sank myself to the hilt. Her teeth threatened to tear a hunk of my palm off, but I didn't waver, slowly edging myself out of her and back in.

She was crying, I could feel the sobs shaking through her body under me, but there was nothing I could do about it. Before I could let myself wonder if she was crying from the pain or just from me, I felt her body start to relax again.

Though her inner walls remained tightly clenched around me, the tension from the rest of her muscles ebbed. A moment later, those little vampire teeth of hers released my hand.

The pain then, not me. That was all the permission I needed.

Gripping her hips, I set us into a deep and steady pace. Her ass slapped back against me with each thrust, and the moans she was letting loose made my brain do somersaults. I needed more.

I shifted her onto her back, tossing one of her legs over my shoulder so that she was completely spread open for me. Immediately her hands tangled in my hair, yanking me down towards her.

Though I was stunned by her forwardness I was in no place to resist, I'd started this after all. So, I bent down to her, exploring her soft skin with hands, teeth and tongue. Various sharp cries or breathy moans tumbled from her, and I kept track of each new reaction so I would know how to cause it again.

"M–more... I need... more!" She was panting now, nails digging into my skin, and I grinned, releasing her nipple from my mouth with a pop similar to hers earlier.

"More what? Be specific with me, Red." She whined and I laughed, slowing down my thrusts, drawing out each deep penetration so that she could talk.

"Teeth," she gasped, "a–and faster. You can go faster." The embarrassed blush on her cheeks was the most delicious thing I had ever seen.

"Good girl," I murmured, and sank my teeth into the crook of her neck, hard.

After sucking until she was bruised, I pulled back, pinning her wrists above her head with one of my hands. I adjusted my angle, increasing the tempo until sweat was beading my forehead. I was approaching my breaking point, but she still hadn't cum.

Wait– why the fuck did that matter?

Annoyed now, I slid my free hand between us, bringing my palm down on the sensitive flesh with a hard slap. She cried out, bucking beneath me, but I slapped her again anyways for good measure before swirling my finger around her raised clit.

She had been closer than I'd expected, clit needing just a few more pets before she screamed, clenching around me. I buried my face in her neck, releasing a roar of my own as I spilled inside her.

I don't know how long we lay there panting, my length still deep inside her folds, her fingers still tangled in my hair. When I finally pulled out of her, she winced.

She didn't protest as I gathered her in my arms, carrying her from the room and to the servant's stairs. I could feel her eyes on me while I walked, unspoken questions pelting me until I finally kicked open the door to the locker room.

I placed her on the bench next to the showers, not looking at her again as I turned the spigot on to warm. And since I didn't know what to say, I left.

Whatever breakthrough we might have had, sealed up tight as soon as he left that night. It's been two weeks since I broke his nose, two weeks since he took my virginity, and he hasn't said a single word to me since.

At first, I took his silence as a trick, and then a dare, peppering smart ass comments at him whenever I could. When one of those comments resulted in a dagger being chucked at my head, I realized that something was most definitely wrong.

His 'hunting' had become more frequent, like the longer I was alive on this ship the worse it was for him to exist. Whenever I saw him, he was loaded down with enough weapons to start a small war.

A belt of daggers appeared on his waist the one day, accompanied by a pouch of pointed stars. These confused me until one was thrown and split the wood of a cabinet beside me. The axe was always strapped to his back, like a warning sign.

And he never took the mask off. He hunted in it, slept in it; at this point it was safe to assume he bathed in it.

But the lethality of his behavior wasn't what scared me the most. It was the robotic nature of his actions. He showered every 2 days at the same time, locking himself into the tiny cubicle of a bathroom in the captain's office. Only ate once a day at the same time. Slept during the same 5 hours each solar night in the damn captain's chair. And, of course, he stalked each room of the ship, in the same order, at the same time each day. It was like I wasn't on board with a person anymore, but an animal.

Despite everything, he kept his word about the 'fairness' of our 'game.' If I announced in the comms that I was about to

shower, eat, or sleep, I would be left alone for
a few hours. He even left the detangler in the
kitchen for me to find, thoroughly eliminating
any reason I had to seek him out. Which I
shouldn't want to be doing anyway, especially
with his newly restored viciousness.

Life had gone back to the way it was
when I first boarded the ship. Before learning
his new schedule, terror chased me every day,
my shaking limbs refusing to allow me to stay
in a room for more than an hour. Now, I
never used the main doors when I moved,
unless they were literally the shortest route
to a hiding spot. And I found quite a few good
ones.

There was an empty chest in the
weapons room that I fit in, if I curled up. The
library had a ton of dark corners and tables
to crawl under. Surprisingly, the Dungeon
had a few good spots as well, and that was a
room I doubt he would believe I would
purposefully go to. Their positions and the

invisibility suit were the only things keeping me alive at times.

If Ax even thought he heard me, he would charge the spot and strike down whatever object he believed I was cowering behind. Then, proceed to destroy all the surrounding objects. The place was becoming quite a wreck indeed, broken glass and splinters littering many of the rooms.

Yet, still, I was empathetic because of the nightmares. I don't know why they started, but now, most nights I would wake to his screams echoing through the comm in my helmet. At first, I didn't know what was happening, as I was locked out of his office and could only bang on his door until he woke up.

So, like any logical person, I began sneaking into his office while he prowled the ship. My suit and his routine made it possible for me to sleep in the corner behind the door

for a few hours, before I'd wake up to his
cries.

He would probably try to kill me out of
sheer embarrassment, and broken pride, if he
knew I've seen him shaking and swiping at
something in his sleep. Even knowing this, I
couldn't just cower downstairs and let him
suffer through this on his own.

Night after night, I would take my
helmet off and talk to him. I'd take his hands
in mine, and he would stop swinging at
nothing. I'd pull his head into my lap and
brush my fingers through his hair, gently
singing a lullaby to him until the nightmare
ceased and he was sleeping soundly once
more.

I was certain his dreams gave away
more than he would be comfortable with me
knowing. They varied, but a popular trio
repeated themselves, occasionally haunting
my nights even when he didn't wake me.

There was one where he would be screaming in an incoherent rage, babbling about the accords and the Roanes rocket businesses. His shouts would ping pong from blowing up my family's home ship to his own, before turning to an incomprehensible flurry of acquiring a star.

The second was quieter, but just as frightening. His voice would shake in a high-pitched whisper, and he would beg whoever was with him to leave him alone, to stop touching him, to stop hurting him. He'd be crying, clutching the side of his face and I knew that in this nightmare he would be reliving how he got his scar. But the third was absolutely heartbreaking.

'I don't want to kill them,' he'd say, his voice sounding so small, like he was a child. Then he'd release a pained cry before repeating, *'I don't want to kill them.'*

Over and over again he would refuse. Slowly, his voice would deepen, until after every shout he spoke regularly. '*I don't want to kill them.*' And with each refusal his body would spasm, reliving the abuse he must have suffered for refusing to kill.

I knew he was capable of it, but despite the close calls I refused to believe he was actually trying to kill me. He claimed that wasn't his goal anyway. In his words, he wanted to break me. If that entailed physicality, he hadn't pursued it beyond the chase, even though he had plenty of opportunities to snap my neck, with or without the suit.

Instead, he took those opportunities to detangle my hair. To cook for me, even now between his rampages there was always a plate in the fridge for me. And when he bent me over that table, he could have hurt me, badly.

He could have been making me suffer, yet he displayed a restraint that this version of himself would deny having. I knew I would *never* understand what he was going through, but I refused to let him push me away.

So, I kept myself hidden. I kept myself fed and washed. In the times I could, I kept him calm.

And I waited.

"Tofu," I murmur into the comm.

It's been a month of keeping her at a safe distance. After getting a taste of her, a chord snapped in me, and I didn't trust myself to be anywhere near her. Denial was a toxic drug, but acceptance was far more painful. I wanted her. And that made me want to fucking kill her.

Nothing in my life made sense anymore, not that it ever had to begin with. I was trained how to kill a man thirty-seven different ways by the time I was fifteen for fucks sake. And now, the woman responsible for all I'd been forced to endure, all I'd been forced to *do*, was shredding my world at the seams.

No matter what I did she wouldn't stop seeking me out. I lost count of the things I'd broken and the threats I'd hurled. But she just kept coming for me, like a chaotic little shooting star, as if she was completely unbothered.

I began roaming around the ship trying to avoid her, but there were reminders of her everywhere. The meals I still cooked for her in the kitchen. The table I'd fucked her on in the planetarium. Even the red flooring and the fucking nebulas exploding lightyears away reminded me of her. I couldn't even think of the color without wanting to sink into her. And her god damn hair was everywhere.

Ludacris as it sounds, that's what was driving me mad the most. It tantalized me, her scent clinging to it, her temper reflected in its shade.

Stray curls shone against the black sheets of the bed downstairs, which she'd apparently begun sleeping in. She would eat in the kitchen now, and pieces would wind up scattered on the countertops. The locker room was a god damn nightmare for me, her eucalyptus and rose scent drugging the air, and her hair was plastered all over the shower walls.

Like a maniac I took it all, even the pieces stuck in her brush. I wanted to slice it with my knives, or burn it; anything to take the edge off. But instead, like a psychopath, I braided it all together and slipped it onto my wrist. A piece of her I could destroy if I wanted, without actually hurting her.

I wanted her close so badly that half the time I tried to sleep, my fingers would wrap around that braided brand of her on my wrist. It had been a month of fucking misery, pushing her away. And a week ago, she started to push back.

At first, she refused to eat the food I prepped for her. I noticed when the two plates were left untouched but didn't think much of it at the time. I was barely eating myself and was in no position to chastise her.

Then the annoying clatter of dishes in the kitchen woke me up the next day.

Upon kicking in the door, I saw her standing at the stove, helmet off, and upper half of her body free from the suit. It was really morbid actually, seeing her half body bobbing around in the air.

She gracefully dodged each knife and pan I threw past her head (always purposely wide) with the tiniest of smiles on her lips. That look made me want to vomit. It was like she knew I was pretending, and that just pissed me off even more. She seemed to get the memo when I lit a towel on fire, grabbing her helmet and disappearing in the servant's corridor.

Then the notes started appearing. They'd be left in the kitchen or the armory, sometimes even inside my office on my desk. I started barricading the door while I slept so she couldn't sneak in.

Her response to that was to leave a note in the dungeon, on the bed of all places. It was suspiciously mussed up, and a pair of her panties were draped across it. Fucking *kill* me.

Some of the notes were conversation pieces, trying to get me to talk, I guess. Those I ignored or would scribble a short reply on before leaving them in the locker room. Others were simple, so I would just say it.

'How old are you?' 24. 'Do you have a favorite animal?' Coyote. 'What's your favorite exercise?' Boxing.

Today's was, 'What's something you hate?' She left that one in the armory, folded neatly atop my father's trunk. Quite an uncomfortable coincidence, so I gave a stupid response. I think I heard her snort, but she said nothing.

But then the handheld in my pocket started buzzing like it was possessed. I yanked it out and turned on the screen, blinking to make sure I wasn't seeing things. Typically, when a door opened the room shone red. Once it shut, it shone blue. Every single room on screen, except for my office, was glowing red. I chucked the handheld into the wall, wincing when it exploded into a million tiny pieces. Well shit, that was going to be expensive to fix.

"I think I might have broken something." Her voice filtered into my ear through the comm, the static making her sound grainy.

"You don't say." I sighed through clenched teeth.

"Ooo a full sentence, you deserve a gold star." The sarcasm in her tone dripped down my spine, lighting me on fire.

"Have you learned nothing while on this ship?" I snapped, "I'll fuck you where and how I please, and then terrorize you when I'm bored. Stop trying to get my attention."

"You seek me out all on your own, Ax."
I stumbled back as if I'd gotten shot. She
added, "I think that's the part that bothers
you the most, actually."

"You're delusional," I mutter, instantly
grabbing a dagger from my belt, needing
something to ground me.

"Says the man chasing me around
pretending he wants to kill me."

"I will kill you!" I roared, slamming
the point of the knife down into the table. She
was quiet for a long moment. I thought I had
finally gotten through to her, but her soft
voice broke the silence once more.

"I know," she sounded devasted, "but
you don't *want* to. You just don't know what
else to do."

I choked. She didn't know anything; it
was a bluff. As I stood there wrestling with
myself, my monitor screen flashed with an
incoming message. The Roane family crest lit

up the screen, and I went rigid. I had to get my shit together, and end this.

22

Ax was silent and locked in his room for two days. I knew because I watched. At first, I thought he was nonstop stalking the ship without rest, but after taking nearly 10 laps and not running into him once, I realized the only place he could be was the Captain's Office.

Finding tape in one of the storage room's downstairs, I used it to 'seal' his door right below the handle where he couldn't see it. If he left, it would peel off the frame and dangle from the hinge. It remained untouched for two days. I had half a mind to knock and see if he was still alive. I shouldn't have worried.

"Alexandria," he murmured the next morning, waking me from where I slept at the front end of the bridge. "You have two minutes to hide." My bleary gaze locked on his door, now open. Then the electricity cut, the soft glow of the emergency floor lights (red, of course) being the only source of light in the rooms.

I bolted for the library but found the main door replaced by the back of a bookshelf. Similarly, the servants' corridor on that side was stuffed to the brim with boxes and debris. He was trying to corner me.

"One minute," he mused in a bridled growl. I shoved the stacked boxes as hard as I could, trying not to tumble with them down the twisting stairs. I half fell out of the ornate bathroom mirror, and was unable to close it behind me due to the spilt debris. The door to the dungeon was ajar, exactly as I'd left it the other day, so I slipped inside.

The glass display cases reflected the starlight from the window, the only additional light to the otherwise all black room. There was only one decent place to hide here, and I hated it. But even with my invisibility suit on, I was taking no chances.

Bracing my foot on one of the leather ankle straps, I reached up and grabbed the arms of the St Andrews Cross hauling myself up. I angled myself so that I was crouched in the divot of the X, my back leaning against one of the arms and my feet braced on the opposite.

"Stampeding your way down here wasn't discreet," Ax growled from the bathroom doorway. I winced, nearly losing my balance and falling to the floor.

It was too dark to make out any emotion in Ax's eyes. His posture was relaxed, gait unhurried as he entered the room. The usual thud of his boots fell quiet against the carpeting, making his movements seem even more predatory than normal.

He approached the bed first, not even bothering to check underneath it before removing the axe from his back and swinging the blade horizontally across the floor beneath it. My jaw dropped open– that would have severed a limb if I were stupid enough to dive under there.

"I knew you wouldn't be that cliché," he said, as if reading my mind. Though the words came out dark, a hint of praise tainted the comment. God, he was an awful actor. He stood, surveying the room, "Just like I knew you would go for the library first."

"Someone's a know–it–all today," I mutter, and he laughs. I frown, "Hey if you were wrong about that last one, I'd be dead."

"Just trying to scare you, Red. Now where are you?" His eyes momentarily locked on the cross, "Can you see me?"

"Nope."

"You're a terrible liar."

"And you're a terrible killer."

"Touche." He shrugged, axe swinging up to rest on his shoulder.

"Why do you do this?" I bit out, unable to help myself. He cocked his head.

"Do what?"

"Try to scare me. If you were going to do something horrible, you would have done it by now."

"Oh, are you so sure about that." He pulled a blade from his belt, idly flipping it in his hand, "Maybe I'm more into the 'get–them–to–trust–you–before–hurting–them' type of game, rather than just plain old torture." My stomach churned, momentarily entertaining the idea.

But as he waltzed around the room, I studied him. The axe dangled from his shoulder like a prop he was forced to carry. He kept tossing the knife in the air, but it was like it was just a party trick for me to see the blade. The stupidest thing I noticed was his hair, half tied back, so that his eyes weren't obscured from view. The way I'd want it to be.

"I'm in here," I said, my self-control zeroed in on keeping my voice even. He paused.

"Why would you tell me that?" Each word was edged in warning. A nervous laugh bubbled out of my mouth.

"Because I don't believe you." His eyes narrowed, gaze sweeping the space around us with newfound interest. I shifted slightly, lowering my legs down the front of the cross, "You want to know why?"

"Pray tell," he snarled, fisting the axe's handle and leveled the knife in my direction, "and stop letting me hear you move."

"If you hear me, why not come kill me?" I whispered. He jerked back as if I slapped him. Wood bit into my fingers as I slid my feet to the floor, "I know you can. You know you can. So, what's stopping you?"

"You sound insane." He was visibly shaking now. I raised my hands to the helmet, undoing the clasp and slid it off.

"Yea, well, being trapped on a ship with an axe murderer will do that to you." The only sound in the room was me undoing the zipper of the suit. It silently pooled around my ankles, leaving me standing there in a plain black tank top and blue panties.

He flicked the blade in his hand, and it splintered the wood next to my head. I grinned.

"You missed."

He gawked at me as I crossed the space to him. I was well aware I was flirting with my death, but at this point, I couldn't care less. I was drifting through space with a man capable of great violence, and had no way of escape which wouldn't bring an immediate, gruesome end to the rest of my family. I was tired of sitting here, playing whatever game he was obviously trying to force happen between us.

My fingers slid over his white knuckled grip on the axe. Gently, I coaxed the weapon from his hands. It fell to the floor next to us with a resounding thud, but neither of us even glanced at it. He only growled as I slid my hands under his jacket, finding the buckle to his belt of knives next, and let that drop too.

"I'm going to take your mask off now," I said before reaching up. His eyes became molten pits of darkness, hands flying to grip my wrists. I paused, waiting to see if he would throw me or get ahold of himself.

Slowly, I guided his hands down and slid my braid between his fingers. He clenched it, like it was a lifeline. Again, I reached up to unclasp his mask, fingers easily locating the buckle since most of his hair was out of the way. I let it drop to the floor between us, fingers gently resting on the nape of his neck.

His mouth was hanging agape in shock, at my actions or his tolerance of them I wasn't quite sure. And then he yanked me into his chest, hugging me so tight I thought I might break.

"Ax?" Her hands pushed against me, but I refused to loosen my grip. Everything in my life had gone from terrible to torturous because of her, yet she was the only thing reaching for me in the flames. She said my name again, her voice muffled against my chest. Fine, I'd let her breathe but not let her go.

I scooped her up, cradling her against my chest. My thoughts were static as I crossed the room in three strides, sinking down onto the plush cover of the bed. Immediately she stiffened, her blue eyes simmering with worry.

I shook my head, not trusting my voice as I laid us out next to each other. My body sang in thanks, muscles exploding with the chorus of aches and pains I'd been suppressing. I'd been sleeping in that office chair since we got here.

Blessedly, she didn't bombard me with questions. She just curled into me (a mind-blowing action in and of itself) while gently humming and running her fingers across my scalp. The gesture felt extremely familiar, but I couldn't put my finger on it.

"Do you want me to stop?" I blinked, glancing at her, and was shocked to see my hand pinning hers flat onto the mattress. I released her immediately.

"I didn't–"

"It's okay." She wiggled her hand out from under mine, lacing her fingers through my hair again. I suppressed a pleased sigh.

"Well, I don't fully understand to be honest," she amended, a frown forming on her lips. "But I recognize that someone made it an automatic reaction. I don't take it personally. That's why I trust you."

Trust. Has a person ever trusted me before? If they did, it got them killed.

"I'm not going to be able to stop it," I murmured, my own hand raising to trace the curve of her cheekbone. "Not for a while at least. I'd rather you not trust me."

"Too late," she smirked. "Besides, didn't you just blab something about getting me to trust you before breaking me would be more fun blah blah blah?" I could tell she was trying to be funny, but I couldn't help but grimace.

"Yea, about that–"

"It's okay," she repeated, silencing me with a finger to my lips. Her brow quirked, "You're not snarling at me this time, that's improvement."

"Quiet before I bite you, Red." She giggled as I cinched my arms around her waist.

For now, I gave up. The chase could continue later. The unanswered messages from my father could be reanalyzed after I gave myself this one moment of peace that, for reasons I would never understand, she afforded me. I coaxed her head to rest on my shoulder and settled in, not planning to move for a very long time.

***

I woke up with my head cradled on her knees, and a pounding headache. Her brows were pinched together with worry, hands cupping either side of my face, but everything blurred against the cut on her lip. I flung myself out of the bed, hitting the ground so hard my teeth clacked together.

"What did I do?" My anger flared to life, at myself, at her for not staying away.

"Ax, I'm fine. I need you to calm–"

"What did I do!?" I roared. Her fingers
drifted to her lip, tapping at the cut gently.
Grief welled in her eyes.

"You have nightmares. Almost every
night." I blinked. That couldn't be right. I
didn't dream.

Alexandria subtly shifted away from
me as she continued, "I could hear you
screaming through the comm… sometimes
crying. The only thing that would get you to
calm down was a lullaby and… me touching
you."

"*Touching* me?" I hissed, feeling
myself bristle.

"Your hair," she explained quickly, "I
would play with your hair and sing, until the
dream ended. I didn't tell you because I
thought it would just make you want to hurt
me more than you already did."

A strangled sound was stuck in my throat as I got to my feet, backing away from her.

"Have I hurt you before? During these dreams?"

"No," she averted her gaze. "I was in your arms this time. It was just an accident, that's all."

"Why are you so fucking understanding?" I was seething, "Get out! Put on the damn suit on and get out!"

"No." That damn word on her lips had my teeth grinding as she swung her feet off the bed and stood.

"I might have been pampered by my brothers my whole life, but as you can see, I'm not made of glass." She gestured to the blood now dribbling onto her chin, sapphire gaze resolute as she said, "I will decide what I can't handle."

"Well, I can't handle seeing you hurt!" The admission tore from me, my vocal cords grating with the effort to hold it back.

She blinked, stunned by the exclamation. I could feel my mouth hanging open as I searched for a way to amend my statement, but found none. You know what, forget it. I'd say something stupid again anyway.

She dropped back to the bed as I stalked towards her, making it easier for me to yank her ass to the edge. Her eyes widened as I dropped to my knees before her, my fingers swiping her panties out of the way. If she wasn't going to listen to me and keep her distance, I wasn't going to keep myself on a damn leash.

I buried my face in her cunt, groaning against her. Experimentally, I flicked out my tongue, tracing the soft skin of her sex. Immediately her back arched, hands folding over her mouth, eyes going wide.

"Let me hear you," I demanded, fingers parting her folds so that my tongue could slide into her.

Her hips jerked up into my face and I used the movement to my advantage, tossing one of her legs over my shoulder. My hand curved under her ass to hold her up as I settled in to feast.

Her fingers were in my hair again, but this time their grip was tight, yanking in an unspoken request when I fluttered the tip of my tongue against her clit. I sucked the sensitive flesh between my lips, rolling my tongue over it harder and began pumping two of my fingers in and out of her hole.

A sharp cry tore from her, her walls pulsing against my fingers as I lapped up every drop that her orgasm offered. I pulled my fingers from her slowly, my eyes meeting her withered gaze as I licked them clean.

Then I was pushing up to my feet, ignoring her sound of either protest or

confusion because I didn't want her to stop
me. I threw a wolfish grin over my shoulder
as I crossed to the closest display case.

"Don't you wanna see how much this
room has to offer?"

24

My existence lay somewhere between his mouth and the weapons on the floor. Weapons he was currently stepping over so he could yank open one of the display cases.

"W–wait!" I shot upright, ignoring the dampness between my legs as I rushed to stand between him and the case. Ax arched a brow, lips twitching as if he was suppressing a grin.

"Is this your way of asking to pick which toy to use, Red?"

"No!" Heat flooded my face, and I smacked his chest. He snickered, hands finding my waist as he spun me to face the case and leaned over my shoulder.

"What if I told you to?" he asked, voice low in my ear.

I bit my lip, keeping my eyes carefully trained on the floor. Technically, he could do with me as he pleased, but he never exactly forced these interactions. I hadn't noticed it until now, but it seemed he was always allowing me to choose how far we would go. He'd done a good job of hiding it behind the guise of dominating questions, or commands to run away.

In the planetarium, my curiosity had gotten the better of me, and I had chosen to stay. But from the Roane's perspective, it was a given that I would stay and endure it. I flushed as I realized that somewhere along the way, I'd begun to want it. A fresh wave of embarrassment had my thighs clenching.

Did he realize I wanted it? Or did he assume I just was playing along with the Agreement and doing as I was told?

"Where'd you go?" His knuckles bonked against my head, "Whatever you're imagining, just ask for it. I'll give it to you."

I shut my eyes against the assault of warm feelings prepared to overthrow my composure, not daring to voice the rushing thoughts in my head.

"I'm just trying to keep up. You flip–flop between serial killer and eager to please at a frequency I can't keep up with."

His hands fell from my waist, and I felt like I messed up. I was frozen to the spot, afraid that if I moved, I would set him off.

I could be reading everything wrong, exhaustion creating fake meaning behind his actions. My misplaced feelings would do little good for me outside of the moments he found me satisfying. And my empathy for him was threatening to carve my heart in two.

He released a frustrated noise, sidestepping me to approach a case further down the wall. It was too dim for me to make out what was inside it– we really needed to restore the electricity. Especially after all the destruction he caused on the first floor. He turned, raising one of his hands toward me.

"What is it?" I asked, wary as I analyzed the dark clump of something resting in his palm.

"Rope."

"What's it for?"

"Me." I could damn near hear the grin on his lips, "I'm going to show you how to tie my arms up with it, and then you're going to ride my dick."

He positioned my arms out straight in front of me, palms up, wrists together. His voice was soft as he explained how to make the first loop, that was the most difficult, but he slid it around my wrists with ease.

Expertly, he wove the rope up my arms in a crisscrossing pattern, showing me the points to check if it was too tight, and how to tie it off just above the elbows. As fast as he had tied my arms, he undid them, the ends of the rope brushing the carpet with a hush.

"Your turn," he said, shucking off his jacket. As he held his arms out in front of me, my eyes snagged on a new bracelet on his wrist. I tilted my head, studying the familiar shade of red.

"Wait, is that my–"

"Your. Turn." He bit out each word, voice hardening. But there was a flush on his cheeks I'd never seen before, and his pupils were blown wide. My breath caught in my throat.

I was right. He was wearing a braided loop of my hair on his wrist! As deranged the action was, it had my heart skittering in my chest. Slowly, I looped the rope around his wrists and carefully shifted the bracelet out from under it.

Surprisingly, it was actually pretty easy to tie him up. Once I remembered the pattern, it was a lot like braiding. Over, under, across, wrap, switch, repeat. Ax watched with clear admiration as I tied off the final knot, before gesturing towards the bed with his chin.

"Can I ask why?" I walked ahead of him, maybe putting a slight bit more sway into my hips than necessary.

"I have a lot of making up to do after these last few weeks." His voice sounded strained, "I don't know how to... express it with words. But I can show it through actions." He lifted his bound arms for emphasis.

"Am I supposed to understand what that means?" I asked, and he actually averted his eyes like he was embarrassed.

"A sense of vulnerability. I can easily break out of this," he said, eyes flicking back to mine again, "but I won't. At least not right away, because I owe you that much."

A few minutes later, he's lounging on his back against the pillows, his arms hanging from the top bar of the headboard. A part of me wished he'd taken his clothes off first. My fingers slid under the hem of his shirt, nails scraping as I dragged it up as far as it could go.

Well, three rounds of military training at least gave me this one benefit, even if the rest was terrifying. At this angle, I could really appreciate all the muscles packed onto him. He sucked in a breath, shifting impatiently, and I laughed for what felt like the first time in years.

"So impatient," I teased while removing my shirt.

"If I had it my way, I'd already be inside you by now."

"Oh, I'm sure," I said as I worked at the button and zipper of his jeans. His cock was already hard, the full length of him jumping slightly as I peeled down his boxers.

"So, why do you feel like you owe me a sense of vulnerability?"

"Is that really important right now?" He hissed between clenched teeth. I paused, fingers poised on the waistband of my panties. He groaned, knocking his head back against the headboard, "Because I feel like an ass, okay?"

"Elaborate." I let my panties drop to the floor, before freeing my hair from its braid. His eyes flashed with primal want as he watched me shake my curls loose. Then widened as I positioned my mouth over the head of his cock.

"What are you doing?" His voice came out hoarse, arms jerking forward, but were held fast by the rope. When he frowned up it, I couldn't suppress my giggle.

"Torturing you for information." I dipped my head, dragging my tongue from base to tip, curious as to what the action might do. His abs flexed, eyes momentarily fluttering shut. I was intrigued to say the least.

"Elaborate," I repeated coyly, before dipping my head. Slowly, I took the first few inches of him into my mouth, sucking gently as I bobbed my head. His hands fisted the rope, thighs clenching as I shifted to brace my chest against his legs. A curse slipped from his lips as I released him, my tongue rolling across his tip to taste his precum.

"My shitty behavior, my forcefulness, it's all I know how to do. And you're stuck putting up with it." He groaned as I took several more inches of him down my throat, panting slightly as he added, "I'm punishing myself by giving up total control of the situation."

"Oh, so you're a masochist?" I muttered, giving his length one last, long, lick before meeting his eyes.

"Where did you even learn a word like that?" The bewilderment on his face was so adorable I almost laughed again. But instead, I smiled, inching my body up his so that our chests were pressed together.

"There's a lot of things you don't know about me, Braxon." His eyes flared, like pits of grey fire.

"If you don't sit on my cock right now, I'm going to fuck you until you can't walk." I blushed, realizing I didn't know how to get him in me in this position, but it turns out it wasn't that difficult. All I had to do was line his head up with my entrance, and within a second, he thrust his hips upward, piercing into me.

My knees quaked under me, and I slowly sank down until he was fully sheathed within me. He grinned up at me.

"I told you to ride, not sit." Playfully he bucked his hips again, pulling a gasp from my lips as he hit deep inside me. "Now bounce until you cum."

~ 230 ~

Finding rhythm like this was shamefully easy, especially with his thrusts meeting me halfway each time. At this angle, he had full access to my breasts, licking and sucking the soft flesh until it was bruised and sore. My breaths were coming in heady moans, body aching for release.

I didn't even notice the excess rope dangling between us, until he closed his teeth around it, and yanked.

He lunged forwards, flipping me onto my back. My legs wrapped themselves around his waist, and I held on for dear life as he pounded into me. His hands were in my hair, his tongue was on my neck and in this position his pelvis ground into my clit hard enough for me to see stars.

"Fuck, you feel amazing," he murmured into my skin, leaving a trail of affectionate bites across my shoulder. I was falling and flying all at once, delirious from the sensation of his cock.

He flipped us again, rolling so that we were braced on our sides. One of his hands guided my top leg back to hook around his. The other slide between my waist and the mattress, fingers immediately toying with my hyperaware clit. A sob of pleasure escaped my lips, nerve endings overwhelmed.

Ax was panting against my spine now, his thrusts getting faster and sloppier. Without thinking, I reached one of my hands back, fisting his hair to drag him to my mouth.

I openly moaned against his tongue as it swept in. Then, arched my back as his fingers began relentlessly circling my clit with a pressure which sent me over the edge again just as he spilled inside me.

"Fucking hell, Red." His voice shook, heavy breaths rushing through my hair. His palm had raised to press against my belly, keeping us together as we caught our breath.

I whimpered when he finally pulled his length from me, still overly sensitive. Gingerly, he rolled me to face him, reaching down to pull one of the blankets up over my body.

He pressed his forehead to mine, the remnants of lust in his eyes fading into a haze of exhaustion. He released a sigh, smoothing my hair and whispered so low I could barely hear, "I can't decide if you're going to be the death of me, or my salvation."

25

Ax was gone when I awoke. I hadn't a clue what time it was, but at some point while I slept, the electricity was restored. I had expected to feel sore, but was pleased that other than a slight rubbery feeling to my legs, I could walk properly on my own.

It took me a minute to find the invisibility suit, my anxiety momentarily screeching that he stole it, but it was just crumpled in a ball halfway under the bed. The helmet was hanging off the arm of the St. Andrews Cross, undoubtedly positioned there by Ax. I felt a smile creep onto my face as I took it down.

As I made for the bathroom's passageway, warring feelings sparred beside my grumbling belly. I had no right to feel disappointed by his vacancy; in fact, it was fully expected. Yet, the less cruel he was, the more I found myself enjoying his company.

I paused, my hand gripping the railing until my knuckles were white. Did I truly enjoy his company? Or was the sex just good? Paired with his behavior, last night seemed deeper than just sex. Though, it could just be Stockholm Syndrome giving me false hope.

I trampled the thought, continuing on to the locker room so that I could shower and dress. Clean, and with my hair in a fresh braid, I slid on a fresh pair of panties and a silky tank top before donning the helmet and suit. The was a crack of static from the comm as I clicked the helmet into place, disappearing from view.

"Ax?" I frowned when he didn't answer.

Sliding back into the passageways, I quickly climbed the stairs. My interest piqued as I noticed the entrance to the library was once again clear and the door ajar. I peered through the open gap, careful not to bump the door open further, and sucked in a breath.

Ax was at the far end of the room, shirtless, sweating, and with a tool belt strapped around his waist. His mask was nowhere to be seen, and all that dark hair was pulled back into a messy bun to keep it out of his eyes.

This was the calmest I'd ever seen him, not a hint of ferocity or suggestiveness in his eyes. Then I noticed he had headphones on, which explained why he didn't respond to me when I called out.

Oblivious to my presence, he turned and picked up a wireless drill. The room was filled with haphazard piles of broken furniture; the full collection of things he'd destroyed in the past month. Whirring the tool to life, he squatted down to screw the leg of a bench back into the seat.

Despite the barley-controlled chaos, the rest of the space was impeccable. Every bookshelf his axe had taken out had been repaired. The books that had fallen or been thrown, had carefully been reshelved. Splinters and shattered glass had been swept away. Papers had been re-stacked and were clamped together to prevent further disorganization.

Once all the legs were set on the bench, he slid it across the floor to stop under one of the desks. That's when a frown pulled at his lips. He glanced straight at me, eyes narrowing slightly as he tried to discern whether I was there or not. I stifled a giggle, realizing he would probably throw quite the violent fit if he knew he was caught doing something nice.

I decided to spare him and backed out of the doorway. Giving into my growling stomach, I jogged down the corridor to the kitchen. The sound of the drill sounded behind me again just before the door swished shut.

I took off my helmet, stomach leaping at the scent of freshly cooked meat in the air. A plate of pork, glazed carrots and seasoned rice waited for me on the stove, still warm. My stomach did another backflip, one that had nothing to do with the food.

'Send that woman's head home on a spike or the food will stop coming.'

Even the treaty couldn't stop my father's bloodlust, despite him having no right over Alexandria. I dared not stay after she fell asleep last night, not wanting another unknown nightmare to cause me to hurt her.

After restoring the electricity, I took stock of just how much damage I had done the past few weeks. Countless items were beyond repair and found themselves floating through space in our wake. What I could fix though, I gathered. I'd removed the knives from my belt, retrieving the tools I thought necessary from the small repair closet on D deck and slowly worked throughout the night.

When the day lights clicked on, I picked up my pace, suddenly aware that if she walked in on me fixing the shit I broke trying to scare her, I had no explanation. Every few minutes, I glanced toward the passageway door, wondering if she was awake, wondering if she was still wearing that stupid suit to play with me.

As the hours piled on, sleep started to nag at me, but I shoved it off. Hiding the tool belt, I retreated to the kitchen, prepping a quick meal and drinking water laced with energy-boosting vitamins to stay awake. There was no sign of her yet, but I made an extra plate anyway before getting back to work.

The work kept me from worrying, and from getting aggravated. So long as my hands were moving, I could think shit through without setting myself off.

My father made good on his threat when the delivery drone failed to arrive this morning. Once every 3 weeks, a regular set of items and food were restocked. He must have disabled the order.

The whirr of the drill drowned out the pounding of my blood as I imagined the idea of giving him what he wanted. She would be dead yes, but then again all of this would be over. I wouldn't hurt or scare her anymore.

Furthermore, my allowance would be set in stone, and the Quadrant under my control. My father would no longer have any influence over our practices, or my life. And her family could grieve and move on, instead of whatever emotional turmoil I'm sure they were enduring due to my selfishness.

My hand was shaking again, and it took me a full minute to realize it was because I had forced the drill straight through the plank of wood, splitting it in two. I cursed, dropping everything from my hands, and stalked to the window.

Why the fuck couldn't I kill her? It's not as if I desired a life with her, or children for that matter. And at this rate, it's not as if we would live long anyway. I'm sure the supply runs were just the first thing my father had access to take away. Worse repercussions would follow.

My forehead thudded against the glass window, and I let my eyes drift shut. *The Ladyship* was supposed to be a home vessel; that's why it was stocked the way it was. If she ever ventured down to E deck, she would find a master suite with an attached nursery. Anything a Roane male and his partner could want was available on this ship for however long they were there.

I refrained from punching the window, not wanting a broken hand on top of my still healing nose. Before the tether on my control snapped, I picked up the drill, tossing the broken wood away and moving on to the next thing I could fix.

I was not a good guy. I was never given the chance to be. I knew 16 different ways to kill her with just my bare hands. So

why the fuck was I fixing this furniture
hoping that it would please her?

27

Days came and went in silence, with Ax studiously avoiding my presence. I grew depressed rather quickly, and then once aware of that, grew enraged.

The ship became impeccable. Everything was mended, washed, scented. It gave me a new appreciation for how grand it was, despite its age. The meals became more extravagant as well, from seared steak with bubbling champagne, to platters of sliced fruits with baked tarts. The man was fucking *baking* rather than speaking to me.

Before I knew it our roles were reversed, and I was the one stalking the ship searching for any signs of him. I rarely ever wore the suit anymore, thinking maybe if he could see me, he wouldn't ignore me.

Whenever I did track him down, he would always appear clean and well rested.

The most shocking thing was the mask finally being absent more often than present. But whenever we crossed paths, he would quickly disappear into the Captain's Office without reply to my calling out for him.

I wanted to see him. I wanted to speak to him. I wanted him to start hunting me again, instead of running away like I was the one capable of destruction.

I went back to sleeping in the locker room, the bed feeling way too big and empty. But Ax would move me in my sleep, and I'd wake up in the silk sheets alone. At first, I wouldn't even be aware of it, but over time, my body would recognize his and I'd wake. I'd pretend to stay asleep though, savoring those few moments and his scent as he carried me downstairs and tucked me into bed.

He also started leaving little gifts for me to find. New books to read in the library. A whole box of feminine products which, based on the order slip, were on board before

I was. Freeze dried flowers appeared in vases in the library and on the kitchen island. He even left my grandfather's pocketknife in my locker. But he still refused to talk to me.

Growing desperate, I began leaving trails of my panties through the corridors. None would be touched. I even stooped so low as to experiment with one of the vibrators from one of the display cases, placing my helmet beside my head so my moans would carry through the comms. He did not appear.

No matter what I did, he would not seek me out or reply, unless I was asleep. So, I faked sleeping, and made it hard for him. I curled up in a different spot each night, under tables, tucked in alcoves, propped in the stairwell. Frustration would roll off him in waves, curses whispered into my hair, but he found me each night and put me to bed before leaving me again.

Such. An. Annoying. Contradiction.

It was clear he cared for me; I no longer had a single doubt about that. It was also clear he would refuse to show it. Scaring me hadn't worked, so now he opted to avoid me instead. Asshole.

So, like any sane and patient woman, I lured him into a trap. I noticed each night he would linger longer, eventually sitting next to me, eventually lying next to me, and finally, after weeks, the bastard fell asleep next to me. And this time, I was the one who left him to wake up alone.

I raced through the ship barefoot, my adrenaline spiking when I heard him roar at the bottom of the stairs as I slipped through the kitchen doorway. He could be mad. He could decide to finally kill me if he liked. He could do whatever he pleased later, because right now he was too late.

I flung open the captain's door, clicking all five locks into place a full minute before his fist pounded against the door.

"Alexandria!" There was not a flicker of care in his voice. He was screaming in pure, raw rage.

I tuned him out, quickly crossing the room to turn on the desktop computer system. Something was keeping him in here, and it was about damn time I knew what was going on.

I dragged his chair over and made myself comfortable, opening the various tabs that were currently active, and scanned the information on each one. Most were pretty boring things: food orders, engine logs, repair requests. But there were so many of them it caused me to pause.

The Ladyship was old, but surely it had been thoroughly prepped before we boarded? This many things shouldn't already be in disarray. I opened a flashing message tab, and was blown away by the number of unread correspondences. Each had the Roane family crest proudly displayed at the top, so why were there so many unopened? And why were they all so…

I felt the blood leave my face and raised my hand to cover my mouth. Dizzily, I pushed the chair back, barely making it the three steps to the wastebasket before upheaving up the contents of my stomach.

The banging on the door had long since ceased, which was why a shriek flew from my lips when I opened it to find Ax sitting on the ground outside. His grey eyes were wild, almost scared, as he looked up at me.

I took several steps back, hands scrambling across the desktop until they found purchase on the handle of a knife.

"Tell me," I whispered, voice shaking beyond my control, "why the fuck is there a picture of my severed head in the message threads to your father?"

28

"I'm trying to convince him you're dead."

I blinked, thinking my ears were playing tricks on me. The knife shook wildly in my hands, but I kept it raised to stay aimed at his chest when he stood.

"So, that's your wild fantasy, is it? Sever my head and send it home in a box?"

"On a spike, actually." I gaped at him, and he immediately shook his head. "That came out wrong. I don't imagine it, that's what he wants."

"My head on a spike?" I yelled, betrayal coursing through my veins.

Stupidly, I lunged for him and swung the blade toward his gut. He side-stepped me easily, one arm wrapping around my waist.

His free hand placed a practiced hit to the back of my wrist, making me drop the knife.

I screamed and kicked and clawed at his arm, a fresh wave of sickness rolling through me when I felt his flesh tear under my nails. He swore, spinning me to slam my back into the wall. The air left my lungs in a whoosh, and I went limp.

"Alexandria!" Warm, calloused fingers cupped my cheeks, thumbs running through the tears blurring my vision.

"Are you hurt?" He whispered, bracing me against him as his hands shifted to my spine, checking me. "I tried to be gentle. I really did, I'm sorry."

I inhaled against his neck, my eyes fluttering shut. He smelled like sugar, had he always? Was this buried under the smell of leather and sweat this whole time? It was nice. If I kept my eyes shut, I could keep pretending all of this was nice and not a nightmare.

"Alexandria," he repeated, softer. His fingers wound into my hair, trying to pull me away, but I held fast, arms swinging around his neck as I bit his throat.

He stiffened instantly, even his breath halted. The only sign of him actually being real and alive was his quickening heart rate against my tongue. I was going mad, truly, utterly mad. That was the only explanation.

His hand closed around my elbow, but I did not release my hold with my teeth. In the lightest of touches, his fingers traced up to lace with mine. Squeezing my hand in his, he bent my wrist back, exposing my own pulse to his waiting mouth.

I gasped, releasing my hold on his neck as his teeth gently sank into the sensitive flesh. His tongue skirted out over my veins, causing goosebumps to litter my skin. Slowly, my eyes refocused, my breaths evened out, and I found the courage to look up at him. His grey eyes revealed nothing, but I could tell he wasn't angry.

"You calm down?" His voice came out huskier than before, and he dropped my hand back to my side.

"The picture," I pressed, feeling my heartbeat tick up a notch again.

"Mhm, that." He sighed, leaning back against the table. "Ever hear of photo rendering imagery?" I blinked.

"Is it like… an editor?"

"Yes." He nodded, "I took an image I had of a previous assignment and plastered your debutant photo on it." A laugh bubbled from my lips before I could help it. But the look on his face– he was dead serious.

"Why?" I asked, leaning back against the wall again so I wouldn't collapse.

"Because my father wants your head on a spike, and I was trying to convince him you were already dead. I don't exactly have a spare human head laying around here that I can glue a red wig on and pretend is you."

"Not that," I waved a hand. "Why are you trying to convince him I'm dead instead of just killing me?"

A single crease appeared on his forehead, "Are you asking me to kill you?"

"You're dodging the question." I bent my knees, giving into the lightheadedness and slid down until my butt hit the floor. Resting my forehead against my peaked knees to hide my face, I let my eyes drift shut briefly. He sighed, and I heard him shifting to sit on the floor across from me.

"What the hell is going on, Braxon?" My voice sounded airy, even to me.

After several moments of deafening quiet, I opened my eyes again to find his own. His gaze revealed so much buried grief that if I wasn't already sitting, I'm certain I would have hit the floor. Finally, he opened his mouth to speak, but then an alarm wailed, and the lights turned red.

An alarm wailing drowned out anything I might have shared with her. I leapt to my feet, tapping the monitors on the table, trying to figure out which part of the ship was failing.

Over the past few weeks, the ship's age was getting the best of it. Which wouldn't be a problem if I could get it maintenanced. But no matter how much I paid, no new parts or repairmen came. Uncannily, the sellers disappeared once the orders were placed. Same with the food; with everything.

In my father's latest message, he was composing poetry about how a son was a son, despite first-born merits or not. My 'proof' clearly hadn't convinced him that Alexandria was dead. Not without flesh. And now, the only way for him to get it, was to pick up her body once all signs of life on this ship ceased.

The monitor was flashing red, but there were no alerts from the engine. Nothing from the oxygen or the water systems either. There was just a single, flashing outdoor video feed.

"Where's your suit?" I yelled over the alarm.

"What?" Alexandria had cupped her hands over her ears and was still across the room. I stalked away from the monitor, grabbing her by the shoulders.

"Your suit!" I yelled in her face. Her eyes flickered with recognition, "Put it on. Now!"

"Why?" The ship jerked to a halt, causing both of us to fly across the room. I grabbed her midair, yanking her against me and twisting just before we collided with the wall. I sunk us to the floor, my hands sweeping across her ribs and arms, making sure nothing had broken.

"Jetson," I ground out against her ear. Fear had carved its way across her lovely features as she sat back. It took no more urging to get her up and bolting for the door.

I dragged myself back to the table, the video feed on the screen showing the magnet grapple he launched had hit smack dab against the bridge. He was suspended in space, the rappelling mechanism slowly pulling him up to board.

I pulled on my boots, sliding as many blades as I could into the belt at my waist and tugged on my leather jacket just as the airlock outside was triggered. She better be in that fucking suit by now and not do anything stupid. I snapped my mask in place before exiting the office, the airlock across from me hissing as my brother opened the door.

"Do you know how many clauses of the Agreement you're breaking, Jetson?"

I didn't bother to raise my voice over the alarms blaring around us. He knew. The semi-automatic rifle slung on his shoulder was proof of it.

I haven't run faster in my life, taking the last five stairs at a leap before bursting into the locker room. Alarms blared even down on this level, making my fingers shake as I located the suit and zipped it up. Braxon's voice filtered through the comm in my helmet, something about his brother breaking the agreement.

"I'm in the suit." With the overhead speakers preoccupied by the alarms, my voice would only carry through the comms in his mask. He grunted, relieving the panicked thought that he hadn't put it on, but did nothing else to acknowledge that he heard me. Jetson was saying something, but I couldn't hear him over the alarms.

"Oh, that's horse shit, and you know it." Braxon cut him off. A few more minutes went by, and finally the alarms quieted. I released a breath I didn't know I was holding, only to suck in a new one when Jetson says,

"If there's no body, I'm not going to be able to talk father out of it."

"You seriously want a body?" I had never heard that much venom in Ax's voice. Despite the words not being aimed at me, I felt myself cowering against the wall as he growled, "I sent both of you images of the body weeks ago. Then launched it into space shortly after because I don't share your taste for necrophilia."

I gasped, unable to help it. If I had been gifted to Jetson, would he seriously have…

"Don't hate on it until you try it brother." Jetson laughed, cruel and dark. A stone dropped in the pit of my stomach at the sound. He would, he most certainly would.

"If I didn't know any better," he continued, "I'd assume you pumped her full of a couple puppies by now and are just waiting to kill her till then.”

“But you do know better,” Ax said, but there was a new sense of urgency in his tone as he demanded, “Now get the fuck off my ship.”

“No can do, brother.” I heard the tell–tale click of a gun being cocked at the ready and jumped to my feet.

“Braxon!” I hissed.

“She’s. Not. Here.” I could almost imagine him sweeping his arm out in a mocking gesture as he said, “Feel free to search.”

“Finders keepers,” Jetson laughed again, “and boy, do I have plans for when I find her.”

I screamed hearing the shot ring out through the comms, hands flying up in an effort to cover my ears, but smacking against my helmet instead.

"Braxon!?" I screamed, a sob tearing out of my throat when I didn't get a reply. I heard some shuffling, and then a loud static pop before Jetson's laughter filtered directly into my ears.

"Hello, Alexandria." I knew he could hear me crying, but I couldn't stop. I opened the passageway door and launched down the staircase all the way to the bottom of E deck.

"Y'know, we could come to an arrangement. You are a gifted daughter, after all. If you agree to be my gift, I'll show you some mercy and grant you a painless death, for the little price of fucking you until all your holes bleed."

"You're a monster," I forced out, my voice shaking as I threw my weight against the door and pushed inside.

"I'm a businessman, sweetheart." Jetson clicked his tongue impatiently.

I've never come down this far before, but I'm desperate to get as much distance between myself and the man upstairs. Which is why I'm stunned to find myself standing in the entrance of a nursery.

The room is full of dust, clearly having not been used for at least a century. There are stacks of vintage toys in the corner, a shelf with rows of picture books and records, and old, wrinkled dolls in a dilapidated crib. The scene is so creepy, it's like I'm in one of those old–fashioned horror movies Xavier used to make me watch with him.

The door at the top of the stairwell creaks open and bullets rain down from overhead. I swing the nursery door shut, taking precious seconds to close it behind me as quietly as possible before backing up to the other side of the room.

My back hits the skinny, folding closet doors, hands scrabbling for the knob to pull them open. I crawl inside, putting my back to the wall, and stick my fingers underneath the wooden paneling to pull them shut in front of me.

"Now, this room would have been fun." Jetson releases a strangled breath, "God having you strung up on that cross to whip you would be so fucking hot."

The St. Andrews Cross. A shiver wracks down my spine. Not once did I fear that thing until now. More gunshots echo through the comm in my ear as Jetson works his way through each room.

Disgustingly, he pockets a pair of my panties for himself, making sure I could hear him inhaling against the cloth. I bite my tongue, resisting the urge to tell him that they're all clean.

Suddenly, shots are ringing out in the room next to me, and I yelp. He snickers.

"Oh, baby I'm close, aren't I? Go ahead, bark like a bitch and let me know where you're at." I begin to shake as the door gets kicked in, and Jetson stalks into the room, laughing manically. Through the crack between the closet doors, I can see he's wearing Braxon's mask, and that pulls another quiet sob from me.

"Y'know, I thought the sex room upstairs would have been perfect, but I like your thought process. This is definitely the right place to breed your bitch cunt."

He yanks open the closet doors, and it's all I can do to not scream as the barrel of the gun comes level with my head.

He can't see me he can't see me he can't see me he can't–

Jetson staggers forward, head lolling before separating from his body with a sick sucking noise. It drops to the carpet in front of my toes, blood spraying the legs of my suit.

Before I can scream, his body, which still hovered in the air in front of me, is shoved out of the way and Braxon is reaching

for me.

"I've got you," I mutter, stripping the suit off her, not caring if I damage it. She's shaking hard enough to make her own teeth chatter, but she doesn't fight me.

The axe was the closest thing I could grab when I came to. It was propped just on the inside of the door, about a foot away. Swinging it almost knocked me out again as the bullet was still stuck in my shoulder.

I let it drop to the floor before I reached for her, the blood on her legs being the only sign she was actually in that damn tiny closet. Such a stupid, predictable place, but I couldn't care less. It was way too fucking close of a call, but she was safe.

After one final yank on the suit, her legs were free, and I slid my good arm around her waist, pulling her up against me. She latched both her arms around my neck, openly sobbing against my chest.

"Sweetheart, I need you to walk for me, okay? Can you do that?" Her shaking just grew worse, so I took that as a no. "It's alright, I've got you." I repeat, crouching to press my shoulder against her waist. "Close your eyes Red, don't look at him."

I had no idea if she listened to me or not, but I wasn't keeping her in that room for a second longer than I had to. I kneeled in front of her, my good arm quickly circling her hips before I heaved upright, draping her body over my shoulder. It wasn't how I wanted to carry her out of here, but with the bullet still lodged in my other arm it was the best I could do.

Her cries subsided as I maneuvered us through the next two rooms, the master suite and bath, before kicking open the door to the infirmary.

"How are we doing, Red?" I asked, heartbeat kicking up a notch thinking she might have fainted.

"I'm okay." Her voice wobbled, but I still breathed a sigh of relief. I bent, gently sliding her off of my shoulder and onto one of the cots. "But you're bleeding." She added, her gaze flicking down to my bloodstained jacket..

"He missed," I said, trying to reassure her. In reality, I barely dodged it, and got very lucky. She didn't need to know that though. And now that she was safe, the pain finally radiated through my body like flaming acid.

I resisted the urge to sink to the floor, forcing myself to trudge to the medicine cabinet. After a few minutes of rifling through the contents, I had a pair of forceps and a bottle of disinfecting wound wash.

"Do you need help?" Her voice filtered over my shoulder. I glanced at her sidelong.

"How squeamish are you?"

"I just watched you decapitate a man," she said slowly. "I think I can handle a gunshot wound."

I paused, turning to look at her. Her cheeks were puffy and tearstained, but her eyes were once again intense, and locked on me. I ignored the pride swelling in my chest, and contemplated for a minute before asking,

"Can you pull the bullet out of my shoulder without puking on me?" She nodded, sliding off the cot.

In my rush to get the suit off her, she must have lost the leggings she wore earlier. The skimpy, white lace panties she wore already had my dick jerking despite the circumstances.

I tore my eyes off her, before carefully shrugging out of my jacket and tossing it onto one of the cots. Locating a pair of scissors, I cut my shirt off, chucking the bloodied garment into the sink. I rinsed the blood off my skin with a spray of wound wash, inspecting the damage. Luckily, the bullet wasn't very deep, just lodged against the top of my rotator cuff.

I felt her approach before she placed a stack of clean hand towels on the counter. She must have found them in one of the other cabinets, and I took one to bite down on. I turned to lean back against the counter, and finally held the forceps out to her.

She looked uncertain, but took them from me without hesitating. Then motioned for me to come lower so she didn't need to get up on her tiptoes to reach the bullet hole. I shut my eyes when I felt the first touch of the forceps, fire racing down my arm.

She was so gentle with me; I would not hit her. Even as I roared in pain when she dislodged the bullet from the muscle tissue, I repeated it over and over in my head: don't hurt her, don't hurt her, don't hurt her.

The cold splash of wound wash cleared some of the agony in my shoulder, and the tension in my body eased. My fingers were shaking slightly as I raised the towel to wipe the sweat from my forehead.

"Will you please sit down before you pass out?" She quipped from behind me, over the clatter of the forceps dropping into the sink.

Silently, I did as she asked, grabbing a packet of gauze before taking a seat on the cot she vacated. I didn't wince as I packed the small wound, luckily not that deep, to stop the blood flow. I'll bandage it later.

She had remained frozen by the sink, rolling the bloodied bullet between her thumb and forefinger. Eyes meeting mine, she dropped it into the basin, before rinsing my blood from her hands.

"Are you okay?" I asked, hating how choked my voice sounded. Gruffly, I cleared my throat. She was watching me now, head tilted like she was trying to figure something out. I furrowed my brows, "What?"

"You killed him for me." It wasn't a question.

"I've killed a lot of people because of you," I admitted softly, "and not all of them deserved it."

"But your own brother did?"

"Yes." I didn't hesitate, "My brother took great joy in causing others pain. And even if he was somehow a decent guy, he shot me. And tried to touch you." Her eyes flashed.

"Why would the last part matter, if you hate me?" The question hung in the air, like a lit stick of dynamite about to explode.

"I hate what I was forced to do because of you." I worded the sentence carefully, intently watching her every reaction. A subtle pout, a hint of understanding in her gaze, before the quick flash of buried anger. Why would she be angry?

"I don't know what they did to you," she mumbled, fingers nervously playing with the end of her braid. "And though I don't blame myself for it, I don't fault you for blaming me. If I had never been born, none of this would have happened."

Raw, unmuted pain radiated through my gut because even as she said it, I knew it wasn't true. She was an easy scapegoat for my rage, an understandable target for my wrath. A safe place to retaliate against what I've had to endure, and a target to unleash what I've been taught.

But she didn't do it. She didn't force people to their knees in front of me. She didn't hold the blade to my skin. And even if she wasn't born, my father would have found another excuse to force me down this path.

"Alexandria," I said, voice pitching lower. "Come here."

She glanced at my wounded arm, but slowly padded forward, stopping a few inches from me. A pleased growl rumbled through my chest, satisfied by her response. I licked my lips, finally allowing my eyes to roam over her exposed skin.

Between my brother, the adrenaline, and the awareness of her presence, I couldn't fight the truth anymore. She was right. I had killed for her, and for the first time ever, I realized I would do it again with enthusiasm.

The crushing weight of that fact was almost too much to bear. I needed relief. Reassurance. We both needed it, and there was only one way I knew how to give it.

"Here's what's gonna happen," I said, sliding from the cot and leaning over her. "We're gonna go upstairs. You're gonna strip off those sexy as hell panties, and you're gonna be a good girl and not fight me, because I'm injured."

I couldn't believe the words tumbling out of my mouth, but I couldn't stop them either. The look on her face told me she was torn, all pursed lips, cherry cheeks and worried eyes, but I lowered my voice continuing,

"You're gonna let me bind you to that St. Andrews Cross and have my way with you. And you're not going to cum a second before I tell you to. Understand?" I whispered, lips pressing the ghost of a kiss to her cheek.

"You were just shot!" She protested, but it was weak. Her skin was warm, her breaths, though subtle, were quick.

"Yea. I was." I tilted my head slowly, watching her throat bob as she tracked the move with her eyes. They were dark, glittering sapphires beneath ocean waves. Fuck, she was killing me. I lowered my face to her neck, growling against her skin in a taunting whisper, "I know you want to make me feel better. So, why are you holding back?"

I won it with that. We didn't speak as we went upstairs, leaving too many of my thoughts to run wild.

I had a bullet hole in my shoulder that I treated like a splinter. Blood stained my skin and my clothes. And of course, there was a corpse a few rooms over.

This should make any person, certainly a sacrifice like herself, take off screaming in the opposite direction. But she just kept reaching out for me, as I reached out for her. That utter fearlessness; that spirit. It didn't quake when facing even the deepest, most unforgivable parts of myself.

I was a little surprised when she marched right up to the restraint, and leaned back against the padding. But as I watched her strip, the pain in my shoulder drowned beneath the roar of wanting in my head, and I was certain I'd never been harder in my life.

32

My heart was in my throat as I dropped my top and panties to the floor. Then I was freeing my hair from its braid, my curls draping forwards to sway against my breasts as if in some feeble attempt to keep my modesty. It occurred to me how little I cared about that anymore.

He hovered over me, dragging the leather straps until they were snug against my skin. Though I was worried about his shoulder, I resisted the urge to comment on it. The desperation for reassurance was hardly buried beneath the lust in his gaze, so I wasn't going to make him stop unless he had to.

The few inches of air between us were quickly eliminated when his mouth closed over my peaked nipple, his teeth nipping against the sensitive skin. I tried to jerk away, but the wooden frame at my back was unforgiving. He chuckled, and bit down once again, just hard enough to send a shock of electric heat through my body.

He pulled away to tug off his pants, and his cock, already thick and heavy, sprang forward. The raw intimacy of that was enough to make me grind my teeth to keep from whimpering. My whole body was buzzing as he ran his hands up my spread legs. His fingers passed over my bare center without contact, and I huffed in annoyance.

"Patience, Red," he murmured, reaching behind me to grab something I couldn't see. There was a slight jangle of metal, and then I was gasping as something cool caressed my skin.

"They're nipple clamps." He answered my unasked question, rolling the clamp against me again before closing it tightly around the erect nub.

My heartbeat was ricocheting in my chest as he set the other one in place, then leaned away from me again. He gave the thin, metal chain connecting them an experimental tug which made me cry out, but the clamps held fast. Satisfied, he slid his length between my folds, and I felt my head fall back as he slowly thrust up, and in.

It was too much. The angle– the stretch. I released a moan bordering on a squeal when he yanked the clamps again just as he sank into me fully.

"You wanna feel that again, Red?" The tease came out strained, coiled like the muscles in his arms and chest as he fought whatever urges he was having. I could only nod desperately, feeling tears pricking at the corner of my eyes.

He withdrew, and sank in faster than his initial thrust, stealing my breath and making my eyes flutter shut. I felt like my legs were going to give out, but the leather straps binding my wrists held me upright. And the ones on my thighs and ankles held me wide open as they tried to close against the overwhelming sensation.

"And here I thought you were gonna be a good girl and listen to me," he murmured. His mouth grazed my collarbone as he spoke, before drifting higher so his tongue could caress my pulse.

One of his hands slid between us, fingers swirling around my clit, and I moaned, bucking my hips forward into his next thrust. He kept that up, flicking my clit and driving into me deeper until all of a sudden, I was empty and vibrating right on the edge.

"Not yet, Red." He snickered, leaning his weight against me as I came down from the high. "Remember, not till I tell you to."

"Braxon," I tried to chastise, but it came out too weak. He chuckled again, tilting my chin up to face him.

"What is it, Alexandria?" I was unsure if it was shock finally setting in, or the orgasm denial he just served, but my aggravation officially beat my arousal.

"You killed for me but won't let me cum?" I snapped. He eyed me, seeming confused.

"I murdered someone in front of you. I figured you could use a thorough distraction." There was a weight creeping back into his tone, and I vigorously shook my head against it.

"No. You killed someone to save my life. And I'm willing to bet that this is an excuse to regain a sense of control." He stepped back as if I slapped him, which was impossible given my current state.

"I stole you," he started, but I cut him off.

"You saved me." I corrected. I put everything I was feeling into my tone as I continued, trying to convince him to believe my words.

"You killed for me, for far longer than you should have been forced to. And then when you got me, you fed me. You gave me explicit moments of peace. You bothered to get to know me, instead of taking the first opportunity you had, to do whatever you wanted to me. You're not a bad person Braxon." I took a breath, "And spoiler alert: I'm not fucking scared of you."

His eyes were stormy with desire, but they were locked on mine. Not my body. Not unfocused. For the first time since I'd known him, he looked utterly defenseless.

And then he was on me again, all give and no demand, transferring the power he had over me into each careful touch against my skin until we were coming undone against each other.

According to a centuries old Treaty, Braxon Roane might have owned me, body

and soul. But in this moment, I sensed he
became mine as well.

I woke up curled against him on the bed, our bodies sticking together with a thin sheen of sweat. Braxon was out cold, head angled to rest on his good arm. The other was wound loosely around my waist, fingers clutching at the ends of my hair.

It was an effort to move. My muscles were both tight from the restrictions and sore from overuse. Everything was sticky and warm, and I could feel my heartbeat in a few of the kiss marks littering my skin.

I bit back a smile, keeping my delirium in check enough to inspect the wound in his shoulder. Though I should feel mortified, after confirming the wound was still packed and not freshly bleeding, all I could feel was satisfaction.

There was a body downstairs growing cold, and a body beneath mine slowly starting to heal in more ways than one. At least, that's what I hoped.

He muttered something incomprehensible, still half asleep, but didn't fight me as I rose from the bed. In the bathroom, I splashed some water on my face to clear my head. I didn't have the energy for a shower, so just soaked a washcloth in warm water to wipe myself down with. When I returned, Braxon was sitting up, watching me quietly.

"What?"

"Are you okay?" His hair was damp and matted with blood on the ends, but other than that he looked completely fine. Normal.

"I feel like I should be asking you that." I said, trying not to stare at the bloodied gauze covering the hole in his shoulder. He grunted, rolling it slowly, not wincing once.

"I've had worse."

"Comforting." I rolled my eyes, bending to pick up my panties. He released a sound of protest when I slid them up my legs. "Oh please, we need to focus for a bit."

"I can multitask." He licked his lips, and I shivered.

"Braxon."

"Killjoy," he muttered but didn't press the subject.

He slid off the bed and took a turn ducking into the bathroom while I slipped my shirt back on. Through the open door, I watched as he bent over the sink, dropping the bloodied gauze on the counter while he inspected the wound.

"I know it's a foreign concept for you, but you're going to have to let me help you if you don't want me to die of guilt," I muttered.

"You didn't do it. You don't have to feel guilty."

"It didn't seem to bother you when I helped with your nose before." I pointed out. He smirked at me in the mirror.

"That's because you broke it, Red." Fair point.

As he redressed the wound with clean bandages, reality began to set in. I had no idea what we had left food and water wise, but the repairs this thing needed concerned me most. If we ran out of oxygen, we'd be dead long before we starved. I'd taken several engineering courses with Owen in the past few years, but there was no way to know if the knowledge would be usefully applied to a ship this outdated.

And, again, there was a *body* downstairs. And I woke up with Braxon's cum dripping down the inside of my thighs.

Suddenly, I understood why he kept asking me if I was okay.

34

Ax was less than willing to share all of what was going on, but with a fresh bullet hole in his shoulder he wasn't exactly in 'working shape.' Begrudgingly, he led me upstairs to his office, explaining which files I would want to open and scribbled down the passwords for the locked ones. I was expecting him to hover, but instead he went back downstairs, dragging a tarp and a roll of duct tape with him.

To drown out the echoing sounds of bullets replaying in my mind, I turned on the first downloaded file of music I could find. It was something jazzy and tappy, but it helped enough to let me focus on the logs and correspondences in front of me.

He had sent so many, both in and outside of his Quadrant. Work orders to engineers, food stores from both high– and low–end caterers. My heart skipped when I noticed an order placed to a familiar boutique line, the cart filled with so many products for my hair and face that the labels were blurring as I scrolled.

Few people responded, and the ones who did bother to do that much kept their remarks short and merciless. 'No' didn't seem to be enough. 'Not until your father lifts the ban' was a common favorite.

I shifted my attention to his personal logs on the ship, and was impressed by his meticulous notes on our water, electricity and oxygen usage. Attached were a few PDFs, portraying detailed layouts of most of the electrical mechanisms in charge of the resource outputs, as well as their access points for repairs.

Finding a pen and paper, I took a few minutes to compare the energy and resources the ship could hold, versus the power output each source demanded. I calculated those

numbers against the length of time we had
been on this ship, to get a better estimation of
what we really had left.

I was left staring at distressingly low
numbers. When all was said and done, we
had a month left of water, less than that in
food, and about two and a half months
oxygen. But that wasn't the biggest concern.

We had no fuel. I checked the numbers
three times before I stood, beginning to pace.
The Ladyship was towed behind the Roane
home vessel, but according to the logs, only
had a third of its tank filled when Ax and I
set off into the void. I knew that once we were
within the Gallanx Quadrant the engine
would be cut to idle, but I didn't know we
would be sitting ducks once over the border.

Unless he killed me.

That's what all this came back to. If he
killed me, his father and brother would have
picked him up and brought him home.
Instead, he was stuck out here with no access

to food, water, repairs, *anything*, because he kept me alive.

I wouldn't say it was out of love exactly, but I can't believe it only came down to sexual appeal. There had to be something else going on.

"Pretty depressing shit, isn't it?" I whipped my head around, unused to him successfully sneaking up on me.

While he was gone, he changed. His typical dark jeans were slung low on his hips, and he wore a grey long–sleeved shirt that I hadn't seen before. His hair was wet from a recent shower, and secured to the nape of his neck in a low ponytail. But my eyes snagged onto crayon blue sling cradling his wounded arm to his chest. Noting the direction of my gaze he grunted, "Figured it best."

I didn't know what to say or ask, so I just gave him my best attempt at a smile before turning back to the screens. I heard the door click shut behind him as he fully entered the office, slouching in the chair I'd abandoned to the side.

"Red?" The huskiness of his voice made my stomach do a backflip, but I didn't look at him.

"I think I know how to fix the oxygen problem," I muttered, ignoring the feeling of his fingers resting on my hip. "If I readjust the wiring so the distribution system only releases oxygen in the rooms we use most, I could triple the amount of time before it runs out."

"Two problems," he murmured, his hand gripping mine and guiding me down to perch in his lap. I ignored the obvious erection beneath me, gripping the arms of the chair in frustration.

"One," his breath hit my ear, "all your education and skills were based on current tech systems. Thanks to the damn Treaty and its traditions, the wiring in this ship hasn't been redone for probably 100 years. You wouldn't know right from left. And two, you have to be outside the ship to access it. Ideally, in a loading dock, inside another vessel."

I bit my bottom lip in frustration, moving to stand, but his good arm instantly snatched me around the waist. "I've repaired everything we have access to from the inside." The edge to his voice gone as his lips brushed the crook of my neck. "I'm sorry."

I needed to stand, to move, to *do* something. My frustration was making my blood boil to the point that angry tears were brimming in the corners of my eyes. Ax cupped my cheek, but I yanked my face away, quickly swiping my eyes myself, and this time he let me go. I stalked back to the center monitor, drumming my nails against the tabletop as I glared at the screen.

"Is it correct to assume that your father monitors all the messages sent and received to your inbox?" I asked.

"Hell if I know, but I wouldn't put it past him."

I drummed my fingers on the table, weighing the consequences, but snapped anyways. I was tired of being afraid. Yanking the keyboard closer to me, I opened a new message window and started typing.

The stars have burned out,

And twin comets met

Floating on a plain of brilliant jet.

A lost sky fell,

Space a blackened sun,

The night's second moon has set.

"Alexandria?" I paused briefly, fingers hovering over the keys. By now, he had abandoned the chair, coming to lean over my shoulder. His mouth was set in a hard, thin line, eyes darting across the lines of text.

"It's a coded message." I say quietly, quickly addressing it to the account number I had memorized since I was four years old.

After a moment more of hesitation, I clicked send. "I know it's a long shot, but I refuse to sit here and do nothing. So, I'm playing my ace."

"A coded message?" Ax's tone was incredulous. My vision blurred as he spun me to face him.

"You expect me to believe you've never heard of them? Mr. 'I'm a trained assassin?'" I huff and cross my arms, "I know it may have been easy to forget, but I *am* the only daughter to an extremely powerful family. Precautions and plans were set in place for emergencies."

"Then why didn't you send this out the first chance you got?" His question came out in a growl, and the hand clenching my waist tightened significantly. My eyes narrowed.

"That right there. Even if I tried to flee, I don't think you would have let me get far. Besides," I avert my gaze, the memory of the fear and helplessness of those first few days making my voice weaker, "it was my duty to uphold my end of the Agreement. I wasn't about to subject my family, or our people, to whatever you and your father may have unleashed if I was a coward and ran away."

He scoffed, yanking me flush against his chest. I started to protest, trying to curl away from the sling on his arm, but he just slunk the other around my waist, sealing us together. Gently he shushed me, tucking my head under his chin so that my face was buried in his neck. The infamous killer, Braxon Roane, was hugging me like I was the most precious thing in the galaxy.

"First of all," his voice came out muffled against my hair, "regardless of how I felt about you, I never had any intention of hurting your family or your people."

I felt a shudder of relief rock through my body, not knowing how much I needed to hear those words until he said them. His lips grazed my temple as he added, "And for what it's worth, I'm glad you didn't use your ace to run away from me."

He kissed me then, softly, but still all consuming. Curling against him, I sent a silent prayer out into the cosmos, hoping that my Hail Mary would work.

35   BRAXON

What couldn't this woman do?

Cook. She couldn't fucking cook if our lives were on the line.

After she sent that message, we were up late into the solar night with her blabbering away about mechanics, physics, and engineering propositions, all of which were lost in a cluster–fuck inside my head. The only thing I clearly understood was everything she was hypothesizing could lengthen the ship's life as it was. Unfortunately, the ship should be docked for her to even try.

After an especially fiery moment where her face nearly matched the shade of her hair, I ended up dragging her out of the damn office, away from the logs and the problems and the solutions she couldn't put into practice. Because there was no way in hell I was risking letting her going outside the ship in the suit that she had.

That suit which made her invisible.

In space.

Alone, because it was the only suit on this damn hunk of metal.

We never got a reply to her coded message. The more days that went by, the more agitated she got about it. She tried to hide it, but I could tell. This woman had so many tells.

When she was stressed, she couldn't sit still. Anxious, she'd twirl her hair. Pissed as hell, she'd stomp her foot. Horny, would be chewing her lip or the inside of her cheek, like her mouth would be trying to ask for what she wanted but her brain wouldn't let the words come out.

Despite our situation, this was probably the least amount of stress I'd felt in my whole life. I wasn't constantly hounded by the memories of forcing blades through people's skulls, bones breaking under my hands, or pouring acid down someone's throat while they were still breathing. I still got the flashbacks sure, and woke up with her cradling my head in her lap from nightmares I didn't remember, but being near her was enough to run most of those god damn monsters back into their hellholes.

I could feel the tension in my body releasing too, the aches in my back and shoulders making me realize just how alert I always was. My jaw clicked when I ate, and my teeth were sore from the grinding I'd been doing for at least the last decade, but I felt it ebbing away.

She was adamant that I focus on recovering, even though I ditched the sling in less than a week. At this point the wound would heal itself, there was nothing more I could do for it but wait. Still, I appeased her requests, only checking the message logs (four times a day) and cooking. While my chores became limited to that, she was a million miles ahead of me.

Last night, she diverted all our remaining water to the first floor by turning off the call valves in each of the downstairs bathrooms, the locker room, and the infirmary. Now the water cycled between the small bathroom tucked into the back of my office and the kitchen sink. She said this would extend the longevity of the ships plumbing, and keep the water pressure up until we ran out completely.

She also managed to divert the oxygen to only the upper deck of the ship without having to go outside. Turns out, on my worst rampage down the servants' corridor, I had torn off most of the metal wall casing only a few feet from the control panel operating the oxygen tank. While the main access point was built to reach from outside the ship, I'd left a hole in the wall large enough for her to wiggle into. With a flashlight, she had just enough light and room to rewire it from the inside.

She was single-handedly keeping us afloat in this metal coffin, when she could have been long gone by now. Safe.

At this point, I couldn't care less about my own well-being. Death had been coming for me for a long time, and I knew better than thinking I could outrun it forever. It was her being stuck here with me, which caused my anxiety to spike.

So, I checked for any message replies, and I cooked what little food we had left. And I fucked her senseless to keep her mind off what was going on. Losing myself in her scent and her skin until we were both spent.

She deserved more than that, but I didn't know how else to give it. And nothing solidified that fact for me more than her bursting into the kitchen one morning in tears, dragging me onto the deck to stare out into open space.

Far off in the distance, a new light had appeared. Not a star. The Thorne family

vessel was had breached the Gallanx
Quadrant boarder.

"They will try to kill me."

I paused my frenzied packing, hands still hovering over the open bag. Since spotting my family's ship, I couldn't sit still.

First, I gathered all of Ax's personal belongings from his office (there wasn't much) and chucked them in my duffle bag. Then I went to the kitchen, stealing the cutlery and the baby blue plates that I liked.

After gathering what I could from this deck, I retrieved my suit and mask from our bathroom. I wasn't sure when he washed the blood off it, but Ax told me where he put it a few days after what happened with Jetson: hanging in the hidden passageway. Where there was no longer any oxygen.

The look on his face was priceless when I'd opened the panel in the kitchen, alarms wailing and lights flashing as I went

to retrieve it. I might have even laughed if I
didn't need to gasp for air when I came back
with it a few moments later.

At least it was semi–easy to spot,
literally hanging on a white hanger on the
railing. Half the hanger was invisible, inside
the suit and all. Ax went to grab the helmet
himself, finally giving up on whatever part of
my freedom he was fighting to control.

"They won't try to kill you," I replied,
but a doubtful frown was pulling at my lips. I
was creeping through the locker room for the
first time in weeks, retrieving the few things
I left down here before making my move
upstairs. A crackle of static sounded in my
ears, before a sad laugh came from him.

"I'd try to kill me if I were them. I
kidnapped their only daughter."

"One, you didn't kidnap me. I came
here of my own free will." My hands began
moving again, reaching to retrieve Julianna's

journal from the shelf in the locker. "Two, I won't let them if they try."

"As touching as that sentiment is, do you really think your five big brothers are going to listen to the wishes of their traumatized baby sister?"

I groan, knowing he's right. Xavier is going to be on a warpath, Colby right behind him. Samuel would be preoccupied with political fallout. Owen would be my human shield, but also force me into therapy. Leonard would care, but wouldn't know what to do. Involuntarily I snorted, imagining him either trying to support me emotionally or getting stuck in the middle of the chaos rest of them worked up.

And then there was my mother, who never listened to me when things were normal and well. I should expect to be chastised for starting a war, and nothing else.

I zipped up my backpack, filled with the remaining clothes and shoes I brought with me, and tucked the journal safely inside. The bag didn't feel nearly as heavy as it did the first time I swung it up onto my shoulder.

I climbed the stairs quickly, the dim emergency lights making the space feel like it was closing in on me. Ax was braced in the open kitchen doorway, hair blowing up into his face as the oxygen from the room flew past him and into the corridor. His eyes, brewing with a storm, were searching the hallway. For me, I realized.

"I know they're close, but we still shouldn't waste our air." I said, unscrewing my helmet and easing it off my head so he could see me approaching. He visibly relaxed, backing out of the doorway so I could slip though.

"I forgot how much I hated you wearing that thing," he grumbled in response. He shoved against the panel, the suction locking it with a loud pop. Then he turned to me, and that storm in his eyes had built into a typhoon.

I suddenly wanted to talk to him about the Earth, a home I'd never seen, but was fascinated by. Share what weather his moods and expressions reminded me of. Teach him the names of animals that I found adorable, and the ones I found terrifying. Share every odd little tidbit I'd fantasized over as a girl from my books and lessons.

Wanting to share this buried piece of my soul with him scared me more than anything he had tried to do. Because there was no longer any ammunition to deny how far I had fallen for him.

Even though I wore leggings and a tank top underneath, I tore my eyes from his as I peeled off the suit, self-conscious of how haggard I looked. My braid was five days old; I hadn't showered in that amount of time to help save water. There was no way he wanted me like this, so why the hell did he keep looking at me like that?

"Red?" He hadn't moved but his presence took all the damn air out of the room. Carefully, I placed the suit on the counter and turned away, exiting the kitchen to pace the flight deck between it and the office.

Stars glittered above the glass dome, the only source of light in the never–ending blackness around us. My gaze drifted to the flickering glow of *The Patron*, my family's vessel. It was close enough now to make out its shape, though it still glowed brightly.

Again, Ax was in the doorway behind me, eyes assessing my path back and forth. The slightest knot drew together between his brows, but other than that he was expressionless.

"What do you plan on telling them?" I finally ask, pausing my aimless trek to stare him down. One of his brows cocked sharply, but other than that he kept that blank look on his face.

"About what?"

"What do you plan on telling them, so they don't kill you and start a literal intergalactic war?" He flinched. It was subtle, but I saw it. I took a step towards him.

"I doubt telling them that you enjoy fucking me will work in your favor. And I don't expect you to say you love me, but I do expect you to say something. After all, I'm apparently not going to be believed because I'm so traumatized and weak."

His pupils were blown so wide his eyes resembled coals. But his jaw was working, frustration building.

"I'll tell them the same thing I told them last time. You're mine." My heart leapt at the claim, satisfaction curling through my veins until he added, "I can do with you as I please. Including dropping your ass off at home and leaving.”

"What?" It felt like the ship started falling out from under me.

"You're going home, Red." He smiled, and it was so soft and warm and sad that I nearly started to cry right there. "There won't be a war. There won't be a fight at all. Just get on that ship and forget this ever happened."

"No." Tears forgotten, I was swept up by a rage boiling within me in a way I'd never felt before. "No fucking way," I hissed, stalking over to him and slamming my fists into his chest.

"There is no way in hell you get to put me through all of this, and then just abandon me. You might not have stolen me but you sure as shit don't get to just grow tired of me and toss me away!"

He whirled us around, pressing my back against the glass canopy covering the front half of the deck. The air rushed from my lungs as he pinned my wrists above our heads, and I yanked against his grip even though I knew it was futile. A frustrated sob escaped my lips.

His mouth hovered inches away from mine, but his eyes were on our feet. The grip he had on my wrists was looser than when he fucked me, but his fingers were shaking.

"Do you love me, Alexandria? Do you want me to feel that way for you?" I blinked, unsure that I heard him correctly, until he raised his gaze to mine.

His eyes were so dark, not with lust I realized, but with fear. He took a breath, voice shaking along with his hands now as he whispered, "I would light the universe on fire for you. But I will not jeopardize your safety just to keep you by my side."

I felt like a star that just imploded on itself. Hot. Scattered. Growing and collapsing all at once. My heartbeat was racing so fast and so loud I'm sure he could hear it as he slid his hands down my arms and over my ribs, to settle on my waist.

Before either of us could manage more words, there was a loud scratch of static from the speakers above us. I threw my hands over my ears as a high-pitched ringing started. Ax cursed and lifted me in his arms to quickly cross the landing to the office.

He plopped me on the desk before turning to the monitors and sound equipment. After a few minutes of finicking (and one hard hit to the side of the soundbox) the ringing stopped.

"Hello?"

We both froze as the speakers overhead popped once again, and we heard a muffled curse before, "Hello? Alex? God damn it, why isn't this thing working?"

"Owen?" I jumped off the table, my voice rising in shock.

"Alex! Thank fuck," I heard more scuffling in the background, the rest of my brothers no doubt. "We're a few hours away, can you see us?"

"We see you!" I said, crying for real this time. Ax had come to my side, his arms around my waist being the only thing keeping me on my feet. "Oh my god, I can't believe it worked."

"Yea, well, Xavier nearly shit himself when dad's old messenger popped up as active on his handheld. Was in a meeting with his advisors when it did, you shoulda seen his—"

There was more static and squabbling in the background, before Owen's laughter abruptly vanished and was replaced by Xaviers panicked voice.

"Alex, stay right where you are. We're almost there."

"The ships dead in the water. We don't have much of a choice," Ax mumbled, but judging from the deafening silence at the other end of the line, Xavier had heard him. Ax had gone rigid beside me, the trained killer in him assessing.

"Like Owen said, we'll be there in a few hours." Xavier's voice was still gentle, but held an underlying clip of rage. "Just stay alive until then."

"If I was gonna kill her, she'd be dead by now," Ax said, voice now booming through the office. "But you probably already know that, and are wondering what I'm playing at, am I right?"

"I'll deal with you once you're on my ship."

The look on Ax's face said he was about to open his mouth and give my brother a piece of his mind about how he wasn't getting on our ship, and my heartrate kicked up again. Before I realized what I was doing, I landed a smack against his face.

Ax blinked, anger flaring in his eyes momentarily, before being replaced by confusion. He opened his mouth again, but I pressed my palm over it.

"Braxon Roane, I swear to fucking god don't make me embarrass you in front of my brothers!" I hissed glaring up at him, "You're not going to be a martyr and stay here to die. So, either tell me that you hate me, or get on the damn ship."

His eyes glittered, and he released a bemused snort before removing my hand from his mouth. But he didn't say anything. Just kept staring at me with those eyes, a blackhole sucking me in.

"Alex?" Xavier's voice broke through the thickening air in the office. I jumped, but Ax's fingers dug into my waist, stilling me.

"You heard my wife," he said, voice thick with approval and something else. "So, wrap your damn brain around it, and cut the connection. Unless you wanna hear her making other sounds."

Fresh tears ran from my eyes as he angled his head to catch my lips with his. In two easy steps he had me falling back against the table. I sure do hope Xavier cut the connection because when Ax's lips found my pulse, I moaned in sweet relief.

I will not kill them.

I repeat that thought to myself like some type of prayer as I sit, nerves tingling with the awareness of each pissed off set of eyes glued to me.

I press my palms on the table, the same one everyone was seated at the night I came for Alexandria. Unlike then, I'm the only one seated and the halls aren't littered with drones.

Instead, it was the eyes of everyone on this ship tracking my every move. The cameras in each hall shifted with me as we walked to the formal dining room. Servants, cooks, butlers, and every other employee on this ship clung to the doorframes and corners of the halls as we quickly passed. They gaped at me, the monster who stole their Lady. Unfortunately, they were half correct.

Now, with the doors closed to the ship's personnel, I held Xavier's enraged gaze. Before we boarded, Alexandria had described her brothers well enough for me to know who was who. And which would be first to go for my throat. That's why I knew the eldest was serving as a self-righteous distraction. It was the fourth brother, Colby, who already took the liberty to stand behind me, that I needed to be aware of.

I think it shocked me least of all when Alexandria side-stepped her mother's hug and remained glued to my side. Even now, she was perched on the arm of my chair, directly in the way of her brother if he lunged for me. I wasn't so sure I'd be able to keep my hands pressed to this table if that happened.

After being rejected, her mother had followed at a distance, clinging to another of her sons' arms. Cecelia Thorne was tinier than I remember, and pale beyond complexion. She looked sickly and unkempt, with men's sweatpants sinched tightly to her hips and a matching sweatshirt dwarfing her. Maybe this was how she normally looked in private, without the layers of glam to keep up her powerful image. Undone. Tired. Or maybe I was the cause of her current state.

I wasn't about to ask for any details, not from Alexandria or any member of her family. The relationship dynamics here were a rattrap waiting to spring, so I just read the room. Kept my breathing even. Focused on not naturally reacting to the building sense of a threat and snapping someone's neck.

"I don't even know where to start." I swung my gaze away from Cecelia, back to her eldest son.

Xavier had a white knuckled grip on the glass of wine he had poured himself. He hadn't done much more than swirl its contents around. A nervous tic. After moments pause, he added, "I'm not sure if I even want to know what happened to you on that ship."

Alexandria flicked her hair over her shoulder, curls still damp from the hour–long shower we took before crossing the bridge to the Thorne vessel. I had been silently stressing about how we would board, as we didn't have proper suits for space travel. Turns out, her youngest brother had a habit of building robots and drones, and had more than enough available to construct the bridge once we docked together.

"Even if I tell you in 'explicit' detail," the vixen drew out the syllables in explicit, and I could damn near taste her smile as she added, "I'm genuinely curious. Would you actually listen to me, or do you just wanna beat the shit out of him and launch him into space, without a care for my feelings on the subject?"

"Your *feelings?*" Xavier's eyes bulged, "The man is a monster, Alex. I can't imagine what you've had to do or accept in order to cope, but I would hope you were strong enough not to–"

"Don't." The single syllable held a venom I've heard from her before, but it was clear no one else here had. Alexandria was all but hissing at her brother as she said, "Finish that sentence, and I'll let Ax do as he pleases."

"Let him?" Xavier probed, voice losing some of its edge. As he glances at me, his expression morphs from disgust to cautiousness.

"Yes. *Let* him." This time, I did look up at her face, and my balls jumped at the sight of the feline smile gracing her lips.

"You're the one who said I had thorns, Xavier. Did you only say that to me to be sentimental?" Her brother turned away, shame creeping onto his features. For a minute, I pitied the guy, but Alexandria wasn't done.

"I know he's a killer. I watched him decapitate his own brother to save my life. If you don't believe me, I've got the footage. So,

again, I dare you to finish whatever it was
you were saying about my strength." She rose
from her seat, eyes flicking toward each of
her brothers in turn.

By now, Colby had rounded the table
to Xavier's side, but his eyes were still glued
to me. Xavier, for all he was worth, looked
like he wanted to chuck his glass of wine at
my head. I glanced at the other three
brothers.

Owen, Samuel, Leonard. All five of
them looked so much like Cecelia, who was
staring at me so intensely my skin started to
crawl. Something flickered in her gaze when I
held it, a decision being made.

"Braxon." I winced, unused to hearing
my name in such a gentle tone. She rose from
her seat, striding toward us slowly with her
hands hanging loosely by her sides., She
made no sudden movements and kept an
even gait. It was as if she could see straight

into my fucking head, and was doing everything possible not to spook me.

Alexandria had backed off, rising to stand behind me as her mother approached. It was her decision, her curiosity, that kept me in that chair as Cecelia waltzed right up to me.

Just like her daughter she invaded my space. I could hear my blood pounding in my ears as her delicate hand reached out to hover over my scar. My hands had curled into fists, but her doe eyes showed no sense of fear. Just sympathy.

"Thank you for bringing her home safe." My nerves screamed in relief as she pulled her hand back to her side. A bit more curtly she added, "I hope you find it in yourself to be patient with my sons. They're fortunate to know nothing of the relationship between power and cruelty."

Cecelia Thorne said nothing else as she turned, exiting the room without a single glance back. A scoff drew my attention back to Xavier and Colby. The former looked at me with disgust, while finally taking a sip of his wine. Colby's expression though held a familiar, quiet assessment. One of a man trained for violence.

I couldn't help but grin at him as I said, "I think I'm gonna like you the best."

He blinked, gaze darting to his sister who resumed her place at my side. A flicker of understanding crossed his features before he asked,

"Who do I get to kill?"

I released a heavy sigh, unclenching my fists before finally pushing myself up out of the seat and looked them over one by one.

Xavier was older than me but was handed a lump of power he didn't know how to control at far too young. And under horrible circumstances to boot. The second eldest, Samuel, was the face of the family given his calm demeanor. The third, Owen, despite his idiotic demeanor, was the brain behind every decision and all the quadrants knew it.

Then there was Colby. A 'fighter pilot' on paper, but really just a politically correct thug. His training, though undoubtedly more docile than mine, most likely was just as thorough. I wouldn't be surprised if he was an assassin. And lastly, Leonard, the only one out from underneath the family microscope and used it to his every advantage. Five blonde heads, five pairs of brown eyes, five potential allies.

"It's more like who we have to kill. Because he's probably already on his way." I could feel my heartrate escalate, but remained the picture of nonchalance as I said, "Governor Richard Roane."

Jules burst into the room then, making all of us but Ax and Colby jump. Her dark locks were wild about her head, her usual bright eyes sunken in from exhaustion. I opened my mouth to ask her what was wrong, but a cry of relief left her lips at the sight of me.

Before she could continue towards me, Colby materialized beside her. Immediately, one of his arms found its way around her waist, yanking her back toward him. His eyes, which had noticeably darkened at her appearance, lifted to glare at Ax again. Ax snorted, seeming amused by the show of protection. I rolled my eyes, lightly jabbing my elbow into his ribs before crossing the room to my friend.

Jules was blubbering something about how worried she was, casting wide eyed glances between me and the man shadowing me. I thought about telling him to stay by the table, especially as I watched my brother's body tense, but Jules wrenched herself free from his grip and flew into my arms before the two of them could start something.

"When I heard about your message, I nearly burst the windows with my scream." She said, tears wetting my neck. I grinned, smoothing back her wild hair.

"I knew I made the right decision giving you the code. Some people in here," I cast a glare in Xaviers direction, "forget that I'm also a Thorne, and wouldn't have the patience for riddles."

"Yea about that." At the sound of Ax's voice Jules flinched against me, but she lifted her head to gaze at him curiously over my shoulder.

"The second moon has set? I interpreted that as negative." He probed further, and she actually grinned at him.

"Your mafia man is worried you said something mean about him, isn't he?" She whispered to me, and I giggled. To Ax she said, "Don't you worry, it was a poem we wrote, what, five years ago now?" I nodded, wiggling out of her arms to turn and look at Ax who looked more confused than before.

"I was understandably upset and afraid. So, Jules and I came up with a plan in case I was able to escape. I knew Xavier would never delete father's comm profile. You were always sentimental like that." I glanced at my brother a bit softer this time, letting some of my defensiveness from earlier ebb away.

"As far as the rest of the universe knew," Jules cut in, "communications with the late Governor ceased to exist upon his death. So, if a message ever pinged through on one of his old servers, the ship would be buzzing in shock. And then my part would come into play, confirming the poem was from Alex since only she and I knew it existed."

"And then step three, which is probably going to be the most disturbing," I said, gaze sliding to Owen who looked like he was trying to melt into the wall. I felt Ax's focus shift to him as I said,

"On my fourteenth birthday, we put a tracker in me. It's tiny and harmless. You can barely even feel it's there." I raised my hand to the back of my neck and rolled my thumb over the miniscule bump sitting at the base of my neck.

"You did what?" Ax practically snarled, taking a step toward Owen. My brother, to his credit, just shrugged noncommittedly.

"Why didn't you ask a physician?" Xavier spoke now. He was back to that half-shocked half-pissed state.

"Because Mom would have said no," Owen said. Then stupidly he added, "And I was a teenager. It sounded fun."

"Fun?" Ax was really growling now, like a predator who'd just been cornered. "Shooting your sister in the *neck* sounded fun to you?"

"Easy." Colby shifted, somehow angling both me and Jules behind him, "Can't tell him it was a bad idea now that it paid off."

"Actually, it was quite brilliant." We all paused, turning to look at Samuel.

Frankly, I had forgotten he was there. He was never one for confrontation, and he'd been silent during this entire exchange. He seemed to age ten years since the last time I saw him, looking closer to 40 than 25 should. Sitting up with an exhausted groan, he removed his glasses to pinch the bridge of his nose.

"Though I can understand your husband's concern to some degree." A spark of hope flared in my stomach at the title acknowledgment, but I kept my mouth shut as Ax scoffed.

"I highly doubt it."

"If anything had gone wrong," Samuel continued, ignoring him, "you could have been seriously injured, or died. It would have been much safer to administer the tracker in several other places. The thigh, the upper arm." His eyes held an unasked question.

"I didn't know what to expect, exactly." I hedged, a nervous sweat slicking my palms.

"Explain." The edge to Ax's tone had ebbed slightly, but my heart still pounded in my ears as everyone's attention shifted to me. I wilted slightly, my voice coming out smaller than I wanted it to.

"I didn't know if I should expect to remain in one piece. If I lost a limb, I could maybe survive that." Someone gasped but I plowed on, ripping the wound open, "But if I lost the tracker, then I would have no hope. And if I lost my head, well... it wouldn't have mattered then anyway."

Ax was a statue, widened eyes boring into me, his chest barely rising and falling with any breaths. Xavier's anger had vanished completely, and he had gone white as a sheet at what I'd described. Actually, all my brothers', except for Samuel, looked like they were on the verge of being sick.

"What happened on that ship, Alex?" he asked, eyes flicking toward Ax, too aware of his reaction.

"Us being there wasn't any more his choice than it was mine," I said.

I had no intention of telling anyone how we started. Maybe Jules, but right now it seemed she was on Ax's side, and we needed allies more than ever. I cleared my throat, forcing some heat back into my voice as I added, "And honestly? It was worse for him. So let it the fuck go."

Silence fell then, and in it I took the only step backwards I needed to be wrapped in my husband's arms.

Ax hadn't spoken since we retreated to my old bedroom. I felt like a stranger in a new place, experiencing déjà vu but not familiarity.

My bed sheets had been changed since I left, to the pale blue silk that I always liked best, but couldn't remember the feel of. My desk was no longer littered with papers and books, but was for once tidy with neat piles and suitable organizers. And there was no sign of my haphazard, rage filled packing.

All my clothes had been returned to the closet instead of where I discarded them on the floor. All the objects I'd tossed to the side were returned to their normal places. It was like a porcelain version of me, the one my mother still clung to for some reason.

"This feels like someone else's room. Completely unlived in," I muttered, half to myself.

Ax had positioned himself by the window, face blank apart from the burning curiosity in his eyes as they travelled my room, my belongings. Who I was before him. "Are you going to say anything?" I ask, my nerves itching in the silence.

"If you had no intention of leaving, why implant a tracker at all?" He asked, tilting his head. "You already explained that you didn't want to cause a war which would put your people at risk. But you put yourself at risk anyway. For what?"

"It's stupid, really," I murmured, playing with the ends of my hair.

"I'd still like to know," he pressed, taking a step toward me. "If and when you were planning to leave me." I frowned and narrow my eyes at him.

"You don't get to do that."

"Do what?" He took another step closer, "Be pissed that it turns out my wife doesn't trust me after all the convincing?"

"You had every intention of fucking killing me when we met," I snapped, letting it all out, "Or, if not killing me, hurting me and playing with me for sport. So no, you don't get to guilt trip me for creating an escape plan that if one day I could utilize to see my family again, I would. A plan which saved your life by the way."

Ax didn't react to my outburst, his grey eyes a wall of steel revealing nothing. I turned away from him, stomping across the room toward the door.

"All the other women in my family were killed, or never heard from again. I accepted that fate. But I was still just a girl," I said, feeling myself flush in embarrassment. "So, I allowed myself to pathetically fantasize about better endings. Thinking, well maybe he'll let me go! Maybe he'll be different!"

"Oh sweetheart, I am."

Before I could open the door, his palm landed with a smack against the wood beside my head. With a yank on my waist, he twisted me around to face him again. I hadn't realized how loud I was yelling until his face was inches from mine, his grin cutting off my next angry words.

"As soon as you were on that bridge with your damn middle finger in the air, I knew nothing was going to go as expected. Didn't you?"

I blushed deeper as I recalled that momentary lack of judgement. Ax's breath washed over my skin in an exasperated chuckle, "Everything changed. My rage shifted, and I hated it."

"Is that why you chased me around, swinging an axe at my head for the first few weeks?" I asked, sarcasm leaking into my tone. His grin only widened as he lowered his forehead to rest against mine. The hand beside my head shifted to curl around the back of my neck, fingering the tracker gently.

"It was a very confusing process. Falling in love with you. I didn't think I was capable of loving anyone."

I froze in shock. He'd used *the* word, unprompted and completely at ease. I, however, was certain my face was a shade of flabbergasted cherry red.

"Are we still fighting?" I asked, not knowing what to say and feeling more confused than ever.

"If that turns you on." He shifted his mouth to my neck, and bit gently.

"We can't," I breathed out, feeling my back arch of its own accord. "Not here. Not when one of my brothers' is probably plastered to the door."

Abruptly, I was lifted, and Ax ignored my half-hearted protests as he strode across the room to drop me on my bed. His touch was exploratory and gentle on my legs, settling himself between them slowly rather than his usual dominant grind down. The sureness of his movement, the care, made my heart leap into my throat.

"By the way," deftly, his hands slipped my shirt over my head, "do you think Owen's a big enough fan of me to pass along the information for that tracker? I'd love to have access to your live location at all times."

"Actually, Jules has that information. Owen just implanted it. If he had access to where we were, my brothers would have kidnapped me back within a week." My eyes fluttered shut, a shiver coasting down my spine as Ax lifted my hips, grinding against me slowly, drawing the friction out. He released a hiss from between his teeth.

"I'm going to fuck you in this bed until it breaks," he growled, whipping his shirt off over his head.

"Good luck with that," I snickered, "the frame is platinum, rimmed with diamond." Ax deadpanned.

"Bullshit."

"You can check if you want," I said with a shrug, my grin widening. "It was custom made for the Thorne's only Princess."

With a scoff, he swung his upper body over the edge of the bed. A few seconds later, he was releasing a slew of curses which made me laugh out loud.

"Spoiled Princess, indeed," he said, rising to hover over me once more. "Fine then. I guess I just have to fuck you slowly. Thoroughly." His gaze roved over me, hungry and intent.

I propped myself up on my elbows, catching his mouth in a kiss. Instantly, he tilted his head, responding with a fervor that sent my insides blazing.

His touches continued to linger, taking the time to caress me in ways he hadn't allowed himself before. His lips were exploratory against my skin, movements coaxing rather than commanding. Soon, I found myself riding the edge just from his touch.

"You've always been so responsive," he said with a teasing flick of his tongue against the swell of my breast. I suppressed a groan, biting down hard on my lip as his fingers parted my folds. He didn't bother hiding his satisfied smirk, "If I knew you'd practically be drooling for me, I would have slowed down weeks ago."

"Sounds like you were too desperate to hold back." I managed to get out, though it ended in a moan.

"Seems that way," he mused, pinching my clit between his fingers and making me gasp. "Also seems like this is not nearly enough for you."

My inside bottomed out and I was soaring, clawing at his back until my pieces came back together.

"I love you," I gasped out, the words and the emotion bubbling out of me.

"Mhm." He pressed another hot kiss into the nape of my neck, "Don't forget that when I piss you off again."

"Braxon." I groaned, swatting at him and he chuckled. I was not in the headspace to keep playing games around it.

His lips on my skin had been traveling south between my breasts, but he paused long enough to glance up at me. His eyes held an unwavering certainty, a confidence that practically had me cum again right there on the spot as he said, "I love you too. Now spread your legs."

Hands in hair. Tongue on clit. I'm sure by the time he came up for air I was screaming so loud every single one of my brothers could hear.

40

"Alexandria." Braxon's voice sounded echoey, my brain twisting away from it and trying to stay in the sweet depths of sleep. I didn't want to wake up and pop the sweet bubble of bliss we had hidden ourselves away in for the past 24 hours.

"Red, we have company." He prodded me in the ribs gently, fingers curling under my shirt to tap against bare skin. I moaned something unintelligible into the pillow.

"Jesus, Alex, get up!" My eyes popped open at that one. Ax was leaning over me and smirking. Behind him, Leonard wore a matching shit eating grin.

"Mornin' sis! Mom wants you for your dress fitting, pronto!"

"For *what?*" I nearly shrieked, clambering out of bed on all fours and reaching for a robe. I was home for all of one day, and she was already back to pinning and primping and plumping me?

Fuming, I grabbed a pair of slippers, planning on marching straight into her boutique–like room and ripping her head off. Though, before I could launch myself into the hallway, there was a sputtering sound behind me which had me pause.

Turning back, I noted Leonard covering his mouth, eyes bulging as he choked on his laugh. Beside him, Ax was holding himself together better, but still had his lips pressed into a thin line to keep him from laughing. A flare of annoyance flushed any lingering remnants of sleep out of my system.

"You prick," I hissed, whipping one of the shoes in my hands at Leonard's head. He was laughing outright and ducking to hide behind Ax– who just reached out and caught the flying projectile effortlessly.

"And that's my cue. See you lovebirds at breakfast!" Leonard disappeared out the door, my second shoe smacking against the wood a second later.

"All that rage for a dress fitting?" Ax's eyes sparked with humor, if not a bit of underlying curiosity, but I turned my nose up in the air with a huff.

"Again, I know it's hard to forget that I'm a literal *heiress,* but hi, look around you." I threw my hands up in the air, gesturing at my bedchambers wildly, and he finally let loose the laugh he'd been holding in.

"Don't heiress' usually have security at the door to prevent theft, assault, and the common prank by elder brothers?" He teased, crossing the room to retrieve my other shoe.

"Oh, I'm *sorry.*" I placed my hands on my hips, but I was grinning now too. "I thought my husband was more than capable of juggling those tasks. Should I hire someone out? If so, I think I'll get a pretty boy covered in tattoos to follow me everywhere. Y'know, for safety purposes." He growled while I innocently bat my eyes.

"If I knew participating in a prank to help build rapport would lead to my wife hiring a playboy to watch her, I would have slammed the door in his damn face."

"I surprised you didn't anyway," I admitted, and he shrugged before answering.

"He said he wanted to make sure you were still normal," Ax said, using his fingers to make air quotes. "And I figured it would help ease the tension if I didn't refuse access to your brothers, even if there's one or two I wanna punch for their idiocy."

"That makes two of us," I said, stifling a yawn. I don't understand why I was still so tired, but I guess my life the past few months was probably just catching up with me.

"So, they call you Alex?" He asked, a brow raising slightly. It was my turn to shrug.

"They're all boys. It was easier to fit in when we were younger." He nods in understanding.

Quietly, we changed from pajamas to day clothes. It was foreign, really. For months, we lived together without any type of real routine or personal items. Now here we were, brushing our hair, choosing from rows of shoes in the closet, and twice the amount of clothes.

Jules had made it her personal mission overnight to stock my room with every masculine article of clothing or bath product she could find without an owner. And I had to admit, it was nice to see Ax dressed in something other than his usual ripped jeans and leather jacket.

Something about seeing him in dark slacks and a black button–down really highlighted that 'mafia man' vibe Jules had earlier referred to. And with his dark hair washed and pulled out of his face into a loose ponytail, he looked younger, closer to his age.

"I think you should know Colby asked to speak with me. Privately," he murmured as we entered the hall. My heart stuttered for a second, and I glanced up at him anxiously.

"To fight?"

"I don't intend to fight," he said, holding my gaze. "But there's only so many free hits I'll allow him to have."

At the look on my face, he halted us with a hand on my wrist, leaning down to kiss my cheek. "I'm fairly certain he just wants to talk. He and I unfortunately have the most in common, and we need to be on the same page when my father arrives."

I nod once, saying nothing. I have to trust him to not harm my brother. And my brother has to trust him enough not to throw the first punch. My head was beginning to hurt, but luckily the scent of fresh coffee spurred my brain back to the present.

"Oh God," I all but moaned, rushing forward past the dining room to throw open the kitchen doors. "Ryan Simonelli, you pour me the biggest possible glass of that right now!"

"Welcome home, Alex!" The chef said, a wide smile on his face as he turned to catch me in a hug. I felt him stiffen as Ax stepped through the door behind us, but the warmth was still in his voice when he added, "And Braxon, welcome aboard."

"Thank you." Ax sounded utterly perplexed.

I untangled myself from Ryan's bearhug so he could pour me a mug of coffee, adding vanilla and sprinkles of sugar before I snatched it with greedy hands and took a long gulp. Ax shook his head when Ryan went to prepare a second glass.

"You should learn I don't take no for an answer son, so make a drink order or I'll make one up for you."

"Make him a girly fruit juice." I prompted, making Ryan chuckle.

"Ice water is just fine," Ax said, still utterly confused. I placed my mug on the counter, making proper introductions.

"Braxon, this is Ryan. Chef, tutor, glorified father figure. Ryan, this is Braxon, my husband. In my experience, he's mostly all bark with little bite, so don't let him push you around."

"Noted!" Ryan went ahead and added a little umbrella to Ax's otherwise plain drink before holding it out to him with a smirk. Ax took it, finally mustering a grin. Good, ally number two acquired.

When we pushed through the swinging double doors into the dining hall, my mother pursed her lips, pointedly glancing towards the main entrance before returning her attention to the papers on the table. My attention was diverted almost immediately as I noticed Jules was perched in my old seat. Colby was beside her, pretending we didn't exist, but she grinned and waved us over to sit beside them in the two new chairs which had appeared since our arrival.

"So," I said, feeling a grin spread across my face as I eyeballed the two of them. "I was gonna ask yesterday, but now I feel like I don't need to."

"Then don't." Colby passed a plate of eggs over to my waiting hands.

"Mr. Grumpy has always been the shier of the two of us, you know that," Jules said, slapping his arm playfully. I noted how his mouth twitched into a half smile.

"Julianna and Colby made their intentions clear, shortly after you departed," my mother chimed in, stacking the papers before her into a neat pile. "I saw no reason to stand in the way of something I saw coming for a while now." She offered a warm smile to my friend, one that had me feeling a childish amount of jealousy.

Against all odds, here I was. Alive. Married, kind of. *Home*. And she has yet to say a kind word to me or even cast me a friendly glance. No, she only chittered about my appearance before making her dramatic speech to my husband and disappearing.

But I haven't exactly made an effort either. I think during the fever dream of our arrival she tried to hug me in there somewhere, but I stayed bound to Braxon's side, too afraid of him trying to flee or Xavier trying to kill him to even make an effort to deal with my mom.

Slowly, I rose from my chair to go sit next to her. Xavier and Samuel hadn't arrived yet, so this end of the table allowed a somewhat private conversation. Though, I knew full well Ax would be straining to eavesdrop on every word uttered.

"Hi," I said quietly, not quite knowing what else to start with. She turned to face me, a delicate brow arching.

"So, yesterday," I wrung my hands, "That was unexpected and crazy, wasn't it?"

"Partially, I suppose." Her hand smoothed her skirt while she replied, like she was nervous. "I'm not surprised at all that you were able to find your way home. You've always had your father's fire, and resilience. I just didn't expect..." She trailed off, gaze sliding to Ax who, to his credit, was allowing Jules to talk his damn ear off all while nodding politely.

"No one is more shocked by it than me," I said under my breath. Her hand reached to hold mine under the table, the gesture hesitant, and worried.

"Are you okay, honey? Truly?" I could feel her gaze analyzing me, but I didn't meet it. She glances towards Ax again, before leaning closer to me and lowering her voice.

"I know we haven't always seen eye to eye; in fact we rarely do. But if anything happened that you need to talk about, please come to me. I won't make it a spectacle or try to make a decision for you." Her gaze is open, encouraging. I hesitate before finally relenting, letting her in just a crack.

"He's exactly what he seems to be, but is also somehow the complete opposite. He terrified me at first, and that was his goal." I feel bad about the admission, like I'm wronging him somehow.

"But none of this was his choice. His rage and his actions... they're all pent up, ticking time bombs. Built by what his family did to him."

"Alexandria." My mother cut me off with a gentle squeeze on my hand. "You don't need to advocate for him. I know his parents. I see his scar. And I know for a fact, we all would have been dead the first time he stepped on this ship, if he wanted it to be that way."

I release a relieved breath I didn't know I was holding as she adds, "But I was asking about you. Are you okay?"

I honestly don't know what I would have said. I might have smiled and said yes. I might have screamed no at the top of my lungs. I might have broken down and told her every single detail, both the terrifying and the exhilarating, but I didn't get the chance to. Because the ship suddenly groaned, and we were plunged into darkness.

"Alexandria, come here." I was out of my seat as soon as I felt the ship shift under us, striding through the dark towards my wife. She was fine. She was three feet away. They didn't have her.

"Ax, I'm okay. It's okay." I scooped her into my arms with a possessive growl anyway. Immediately, she wrapped her legs around my waist and her arms around my neck.

Nothing was okay. He was here. He was already fucking here.

"Braxon," Colby's voice cut toward me through the dark.

"I know," I growled out again, barely able to contain myself. "Damn it, we should have figured out a plan last night."

"Leo, take the girls to the Governess' strong room, and lock yourselves in. Owen, go find Xavier and Sam, now!" Colby ordered.

"Run," I added, voice grave. Cecelia was protesting, but her voice was drifting away as one of her sons quickly guided her to the door. Finally, security lights flickered along the baseboards, casting the room into a dull blue glow.

"Alex, what the fuck?" Colby yelled, glaring directly at me. Shit that was right; she was currently hanging off me like a koala and she just cinched herself tighter.

"Last time we got separated, we almost got killed." She shot back at her brother, eyes on fire.

"Last time?" He bellowed, "The fuck do you mean *last time*?"

"His brother–"

"This will not be like my brother." I cut them both off. In one move, I got her legs unlatched from around me, then her arms, and she was back on the floor blinking up at me in confusion.

"My brother came after us to make a legend of himself. My father will be here on a raid. Squads of soldiers, all trained exactly like me." Her eyes widened as I looked back to Colby, "I got some things from my ship last night while she slept. We'll need them."

"But Alex–"

"Will not be seen," I said definitively before looking back at her.

"Go get your suit, sweetheart." She grinned up at me, her eyes glittering so distressingly beautiful, that I momentarily felt like I was floating. Then she was darting out the door.

Colby looked like he wanted to shoot me and follow her, but I shook my head. I motioned for him to follow me as I quickly crossed the room, kicking open the set of double doors to the kitchen.

"You good with guns?" I asked, and he scoffed.

"What do you think?"

"And hand to hand?" I was being way too civil about this, and I could tell it was beginning to freak him out. Pausing in front of the walk-in pantry, I kept my voice even, but added a note of seriousness as I locked eyes with him. "Colby, if you can't fight hand to hand, you're going to die."

"I can fight hand to hand," he finally responded. "Now why the hell are we standing in my kitchen?"

There was a reason the chef was wary of me earlier, one that Alexandria didn't know about. I didn't bother to fill her in at the time, not wanting to freak her out or worse, get her mother involved. I turned from

Colby, throwing open the pantry doors and motioned for him to step inside.

After Alexandria had fallen asleep, I sought out Samuel, figuring he would be most lenient towards my request. Not counting whatever stash Colby most likely had, this ship was not outfitted with enough weapons to go head–to–head with Governor Roane. They had gunner stations outside sure, but I knew we wouldn't see my father coming. I'd coughed up every bit of information I had on our stealth ships and tech, and after recovering from the initial shock, Samuel agreed we needed more firepower on board for when he arrived.

Even in the dim light, I could see Colby's eyes widen as he took in the number of weapons lining the shelves. Throughout the night, Myself, Samuel, and Ryan the Chef, cleared out the pots, pans, random bags of flour, eating utensils and the like, moving it all to deep storage. Unless it was perishable or needed to be kept cool, it was removed to create the space needed to load my entire arsenal from *The Ladyship* on board.

Before he returned to his quarters, Samuel took two of my shotguns with him for himself and Xavier, as well as a hunting knife for his mother. Ryan had taken a duffle bag of various knives and saws, some even from his own cooking supplies, to stash in the staff chambers in case they needed them. At my insistence, he also took a few guns.

"Take what you need," I grunted, already swinging my belt of daggers around my hips.

Colby cursed under his breath, but grabbed two of my handguns before moving to the rack of remaining blades. I slid a pistol into my waistband, before closing my fist around the handle of my axe. This ends today.

42

My heart was working double time as I sprinted down the halls to my room. I didn't need the emergency lights to see; I've had this ship memorized for years. In fact, I'd rather all the lights be *off.*

I had no way of knowing where Richard Roane or his men were, and I knew I only had limited time before they would be looking for me. Or for Ax. Honestly, at this rate, I'm unsure who he wanted dead more.

Breathe, Alex. Ax was calm. Disturbingly calm. He was already in action by the time I left. I needed to remain calm so I wouldn't distract him and get him killed.

I all but knocked my bedroom door off its hinges as I threw it open, sprinting across the space to my private bathroom. I flung open the storage doors beneath the sink, grabbing the small zip-up travel bag I had put my suit in. I think I would take it with me everywhere for the rest of my life, then leave it in my will for my children.

I shucked off my clothes, dropping them haphazardly and unzipped the bag. It was easily the brightest, most obnoxious bag in my collection. Neon blue and yellow plastic, which was covered in pink glitter. It would be impossible to misplace or not see because it was that glaring.

I yanked the suit on, the zipper sliding into place like a second skin. Then I pulled my helmet out from underneath the sink. I caught my eye in the mirror as I slid it over my head. Calm; breathe.

I clicked it into place, and I disappeared.

Colby could hold his own, I'll give him that much credit. Our fighting styles completely clashed though. I preferred to wait and observe, sitting on defense until my opponent fucked up enough before I'd land a single, fatal strike. But fuck, Colby Thorne was an ambush predator on a leash.

Earlier, when we started stalking the halls, Red's voice chimed in over the intercom. While I resisted the urge to laugh, Colby sent up a storm of curses. Pride and fear danced side by side in my chest as she all but baited my father into finding her first. It was an impossible task if she had her suit on. And she better have the damn thing on.

That gave Colby and I the advantage, as the raids' attention was elsewhere. My father was a sinfully proud man. He wouldn't be able to ignore public displays of disrespect, like the blatant insults she spewed for all of us to hear before cutting whatever connection she linked. And her efforts worked like a dream.

My father's men were sloppy, and loud. Colby and I both agreed it would be smart to wait until they stumbled close enough, rather than sprinting around corners and shooting blindly. So, with a boost, we hiked each other up into one of the inconspicuous air ducts running the full length of each hall.

I was content to squat in there for a bit and plan, but as soon as there was movement below us, Colby shot out of the duct like a viper. I picked off the two guys behind him with headshots as he dropped straight into the pack of four of them. Before my feet even hit the floor the other two were dead.

"There'll be twelve of them," I muttered as I reloaded. "They only travel in pairs or groups of four, making the total six or twelve. They never mix and match." And, apparently, my father decided to bring double the guns for a civil dispute.

It was smart of him, not to underestimate this family. But it pissed me off all the same that he was this determined to destroy them. And for what? More literal space filled with nothing. I could practically taste my disdain for it as I released the shot into the first guy's head.

"So, eight left plus daddy." Colby wiped the blood off the twin daggers he took from my stash. They were just under a foot long, with curved, serrated blades. I grunted an affirmation, dragging my axe down from the air duct.

"Okay, for real, what's going on with that?" Colby asked, eyes studying the weapon's craftsmanship.

"This is the only weapon I've ever liked," I murmured, lifting the blade. "So, he wanted me to kill your sister with it."

Colby stilled, and I felt his eyes on me, on the axe. I swung it once, slowly, the familiarity of the grip caressing my palm as I said, "I want to deal the killing blow with it, but I doubt he'll let me get that close."

"I don't know whether or not to approve, or call you a crazy bastard." He said with a shake of his head. I shrugged, flashing a half grin which I knew had my scar turning up all kinds of ugly.

"I'm just a psycho with a good revenge plan," I drawled, shrugging innocently and Colby snorted.

I would dare say things were going well in the rapport section, because yes, that ranked above killing a bunch of assassins. The list of priorities in my head is most definitely a flexible thing. But then the loudspeaker crackled overhead, making both of us stop in our tracks.

"Hello, Braxon." I said nothing as my father released a long sigh. "You've turned this into quite a spectacle. I can't tell you how disappointed I am."

"Likewise," I muttered, unsure if he could hear me or not. There was a scuffling sound momentarily, before a very feminine cry had my stomach lurching like the ship was in a freefall.

"You hear her, Braxon?" There was an audible hit, metal on flesh, and I roared. "That's it, son," my father laughed. "Come get her before I take this opportunity to *fully* enjoy her. Perhaps she'll be just as valuable as her mother was, and provide me with a worthy heir."

Colby took off back the way we'd come. As it was his ship, I followed his lead, unable to do much else than try to control the beast threatening to break loose.

Fuck the axe; I was going to tear my father to pieces with my bare hands.

44

The ship was dead silent other than my rapid footfalls and breaths as I ran for the main deck. I rarely ever went up there; I never needed to. But if I could connect my helmet to *The Ladyships* ancient speaker system, then connecting it to my own tech would be a breeze.

Call it pettiness, but the insults rolling off my tongue were long overdue. I couldn't stop the rush of manic laughter as I provoked the man. There was a time my actions would have appalled even me, but honestly, I had no more self-control or patience for the situation. The Governor of an enemy Quadrant was threatening my family on my own ship. So, I took my muzzle off, and did what I did best.

I had fallen quiet a few minutes ago, sneaking selfishly towards my mother's quarters. I was hoping to confirm everyone was safely locked inside, but the group of men milling outside the door had me stop in my tracks and duck around the nearest corner.

They were armed to the teeth, slamming the butt of their guns against my mother's door. One of them had a drill and was working on the hinges. Though their efforts were futile (they would need a literal bomb to get that door open once it was sealed) my nerves were still sending out every panic signal my body was capable of. I was so absorbed by what they were doing, that when the speaker popped over my head I couldn't contain my scream.

Bullets had immediately flown in my direction, and I took off. I didn't have a gun, didn't have weapons of any sort. They'd heard me running of course and gave chase, continuing to shoot even after I'd turned another corner and was out of range.

My blood chilled as Richard Roane's voice echoed through the ship, taunting his son. Baiting him. And then a woman was screaming.

For a moment I thought it was my mother, but the voice was too velvety, not shrill like a bird. I don't know who Richard was torturing, but it was clear he wanted Ax to think it was me. And if Ax thought it was…

My heart was beating triple time, a new sense of fear in me. One of the men just rounded the corner. He had a shotgun propped on his shoulder as his eyes scanned the 'empty' hallway for any sign of movement. I gritted my teeth, adrenaline rushing through me. This was stupid, stupid, *stupid!*

But I couldn't keep hiding. Not when Ax was going to be running straight into a trap. Shaking, I took one silent step after another, back toward the man at the end of the hall. I held my breath when we were shoulder to shoulder, but he had no idea.

With my blood pounding in my ears, I reached out, yanking one of the handguns off his belt and fired it straight up into his face. I screamed again as blood sprayed everywhere and he fell forward, body hitting the floor with a thud. His blood was seeping into the footpads of my suit, and stained the visor of my helmet, but I didn't even bother to wipe it. I just killed a man. I wanted to throw up. I wanted to pass out.

But there were three more sets of heavy footfalls now racing my way. So, gun in hand, I turned on my heel and launched myself towards the hidden servant's entrance a few yards down the hallway. The tiny corridor would have no emergency lights, but I wasn't afraid of the dark.

I had blown past Colby as Alexandria's screams continued through the loudspeaker. I didn't know where I was going, only guided by Colby's shouts from behind me, until finding the literal red carpet my father must have rolled out which led all the way to the Governor's office.

It wasn't Xavier's. For some reason, Colby had found it necessary to point out his brother established his own office and didn't encroach on his father's as we crept towards the door. The look in his eyes, and the quick defensiveness of the words, had me briefly wondering what it was like to hold your father in such high regard that even death couldn't take away your respect for him. Especially since I was inches away from murdering mine.

Four more bodies lined the hallway behind us. One was already dead when we arrived and missing his gun, a sign that Alexandria had been through here. The thought of her anywhere near them had me tearing through the last three, leaving them all but shredded behind me. Colby had put a bullet in each of their heads for good measure.

That would leave the last squad inside the office with Richard Roane. Of course, why would he fight his own battles, or even defend himself, when he had an arsenal of trained mercenaries to do his dirty work?

We took a moment to check the door for any hidden trip wires or explosives, though I was willing to bet he wouldn't lay one so close to himself. Especially now that he didn't have an heir to continue his legacy. I killed my brother, and he sure as hell wasn't gonna place the bloody crown on my head.

I suddenly froze in the doorway, the look on my face causing Colby to scrunch his brows together. My brother was dead. I was a wanted man. And, judging by the silence alone, Alexandria definitely wasn't in that room with him. A wave of nausea rolled over me as I realized who was. Colby barely had time to move back before I busted the door off its hinges, shattering the frame since it wasn't even locked.

Richard Roane was wearing a pressed white suit in the otherwise grey room. He leaned against an old desk, which stood empty, save for his gun resting against the polished wood. I saw nothing else as my eyes zeroed in on the woman at his feet, bound and bleeding from the temple.

"Mom?"

Tears were streaming down her face, mixing with her blood and dripping off her chin. When I took note of her broken fingers, I actually thought I was going to hurl.

My mother was never a particularly warm person, but I always considered her presence a place of refuge. Though she certainly did nothing to prevent my father's cruelty, she did expose me to kinder treatment on the rare occasions we were together. Looking at her now, sobbing and bleeding around the ball gag in her mouth, I finally realized that she probably experienced even more cruelty than I had. And unlike her youngest son, neither of us was built for it.

"Now that the rest of the family is here, we can get started." My father's voice reached my ears, but my eyes didn't register the sudden movement in the room. Numbly, I dropped to my knees, vision banking as I felt the hilt of a pistol connect with the back of my skull.

A corpse dropped next to me as Colby shot the mercenary who hit me, but then he too was thrown to the floor. I was already working my way back to my feet, but froze as my father raised his gun, the barrel caressing the side of my mother's neck.

Suppressing a growl, I lowered myself back to my knees beside Colby. My whole body shook as the remaining three mercenaries stripped us of our weapons, tossing them back out the open door into the hallway behind us.

"Now, what should we do with you?" My father bent to murmur something in my mother's ear, and she released another terrified noise, trying to jerk away from him. He chuckled, yanking her to her feet by the hair.

"You've provided me with sons, yes." He trailed the gun down her body to rest on her lower abdomen. Atop her womb, I realized with a sickening twist in my own gut. He continued to speak to her as if we weren't there, "But one was too weak to live, while the other is too weak to kill. How can I trust you'll produce another heir at your age?

And that he will be one of strength and caliber?"

"The bodies of your men behind me would argue I'm capable of killing quite efficiently," I hissed. That finally had him turn back to me.

Dropping my mother to the floor, he simply raised his gun, and shot. Colby howled, bending double after the bullet hit him somewhere on the leg. I didn't even turn to look, not trusting my wavering sense of control to not snap and have my mother pay for it.

"Why harm them when it's me you want to tear apart?" I asked, cocking my head to the side. My mother was crying again, body shaking as silent sobs quaked through her.

"One's an enemy. Another's a failure. Why should anything but harm befall them?" Richard regarded me with a look I knew all too well. Dark. Devouring. Demanding. And yet, he was the symbol of patience, leaning back against the desk again to reload the pistol in his hand with just a single bullet.

"Well, one is your wife," I pointed out. There was a resounding click as he took the safety off and once again, raised the pistol toward Colby.

"And the other?" He prompted. A buried note of bloodlust made his voice tremble. I gritted my teeth, holding his stare.

"A friend."

I imagined that I felt the breeze of the bullet fly past my face, even though I knew that wasn't possible. Colby didn't utter a sound as the bullet struck him in the chest. I remained a statue, eyes glued to my father as he slumped to the marble floor, motionless.

"Now that that's taken care of," Richard gestured toward the man at my right and instinctively, I reached to block his attack. I succeeded, but the man behind me sank a knife into my previously wounded shoulder, making me roar. The pain didn't matter though, and my father's eyes widened as he realized his men's mistake.

I tore the blade from my flesh, flipping it midair to sink it deep into the gut of the mercenary before me. Ducking between his legs, his body took the shots fired at me by the other two. As his gun clattered to the floor, Colby moved, snapping forward like a python to snatch it up and release a flurry of bullets into the backs of the two chasing after me.

The last one was frozen in the doorway, staring at Colby as if he was a ghost. I snorted; as if we wouldn't have worn bullet proof vests during a literal gunfight. I tilted my wrist, flicking the knife across the room to embed in the side of his neck. As he lay choking on his own blood behind me, I faced my father again.

He'd discarded the gun on the table, and now held a blade flush against my mother's pulse. I felt my skin crawl, my body trying to detach and sprint from the blade I knew most intimately.

"What do you say, Braxon? Should I give her an accessory to complement yours?"

I couldn't help but wince as he raised the teeth of the machete to pucker the skin on her cheek. He clucked his tongue, like he was annoyed that she was shaking while being used as a human shield. Slowly, Colby raised the gun at them.

"Don't!" I barked, not trusting his aim to miss my mother.

"Oh, come now, boys, it's our wedding anniversary. All good husbands get their wives an expensive accessory for their special day." Richard grinned, baring his teeth, "and as you know son, it is quite expensive. To fix. And this time I won't be paying for–"

Abruptly, my father stumbled forward, his sentence cut off. The machete in his hands clattered to the floor as he stared at me, mouth open but not moving. He coughed roughly, and blood splattered the front of his pristine suit.

And then, Governor Richard Roane shut his eyes, body unceremoniously impacting the floor with my axe embedded between his shoulder blades. A soft click resounded in the silence, before her muffled voice reached my ears.

"I was getting really sick and tired of his dramatic monologues."

As soon as I heard the zipper of her suit, I had Alexandria in my arms.

My mother never failed to outdo herself when it came to a special event, but at least this time around I was able to dodge most of her ludicrous attentions. Most of them, anyways. Jules still wound up knelt at my feet, making last minute alterations to my red velvet jumpsuit.

"I'm still blown away that you were able to argue yourself out of wearing the seafoam green dress she ordered," she said, eyes flicking up at me. I scrunched my nose.

"It was hideous." The image of the feathered cocktail dress coming to mind made my skin itch just thinking about it.

"Hey, you didn't hear me argue in favor of it. Besides," she trailed off, giving me a onceover.

I wore simple black flats under the swishing legs of the suit. The velvet bodice appeared to shift between crimson and wine red as I moved. A tight silver belt perched high on my hips, and matched the drooping earrings I wore. They glittered with flecks of sapphire, matching the hair clips tucked into my twin Dutch braids. The blue was an identical shade to my wedding band. The color of my eyes, Braxon had said.

"Well?" I arched a brow. Jules smiled softly.

"It suits you."

Quickly, we finished up, just a swipe of eyeliner and mascara on each of us, before we were out the door. I helped her straighten her own skirt, a gorgeous tangerine number, before we marched arm in arm down the hallway.

"Will I ever convince you to not behave as if you're still my lady's maid?" I asked, eyeing the sparkling rock on her own ring finger. She giggled.

"Probably not. I'm afraid you and your brother will just have to accept that I like pampering my best friend." I muttered something about Colby threatening to wring my neck a few days ago, which had her giggling, cheeks flushing.

They had married as soon as he was out of recovery. It was a small, quaint ceremony void of any press; under the strict stipulation they submitted a *full* press-ready story on how they fell in love. I helped complete it with photos from the wedding, as soon as their honeymoon was over.

As we entered the dining hall, I had to squint from the brightness. Everything was glittering silver, gold, or pearl, from the drapes to the napkins on the table. It was like my mother literally powdered the space with fairy dust. I suppressed the urge to roll my eyes as she rushed towards us, all but dragging poor Tabitha Roane along with her.

The widowed ex-governess had shockingly accepted my proposal to remain living here with us. When I first met her, she appeared cold and cruel, but out from underneath her husband's command she truly was a gentle woman. In fact, the only dark thing that remained about her was the curtain of black hair framing her face.

"What do you think?" My mother released her hold on Tabitha to take me by the shoulders and turn me around the room to take everything in– as if I could have missed it before. "I know you said to keep it simple, but this is our first public appearance in over a year, and it's for such a joyous thing. After all we have been through–"

"Mom," I cut her off gently, covering one of her hands with my own so she would stop spinning me. "It's perfect, thank you."

She gave me a dazzling smile before pulling me in for a tight hug. It was still a new thing for us, the closeness, the acceptance, but she was trying, so I would put in my best efforts. Even if the ice sculpture of a swan on the center table made me want to gouge my own eyes out.

"Did Xavier handle the press though? No drones are going to be randomly squatting in the hallway?" I asked as she released me, and she nodded.

"All are under strict orders to remain outside the ship, only videotaping or photographing what they can view from the windows." She laughed, before adding, "And with nearly half of Braxon's fleet out there, well, I doubt they'd try to sneak in."

I couldn't suppress my chuckle. Of course, he had ordered way too many of his pilots to circle *The Patron*, but considering the circumstances, I decided not to tease him about it. Too much.

"Do you know where he is?" I asked, glancing between her and Tabitha. My mother had already begun to chatter about how he wasn't cooperating with his hair, but Tabitha just gave me a small smile.

"They're both in the gallery. Waiting for you, I'd assume."

I squeezed Jules's hand before slipping away, out through the kitchen door. Everyone was busy at work, but Ryan still paused to wink at me over the dishes blowing steam up into his face. I weaved through the servant's corridor, before emerging into the gallery.

The only light came from the dull glow of the ancient chandelier (a relic from our ancestors on Earth) hanging delicately from the ceiling. Around the room, various photos and paintings were displayed, all of the family. I paused before the only portrait of Julianna Roane, my great grandmother who, like me, defied the odds. Without her journal, the man in front of me wouldn't be in my life at all.

"So, why are you hiding?" I asked, sidling up next to Ax. Rising onto my tiptoes, I pressed a soft kiss to his cheek.

I don't know what my mother was complaining about; he looked absolutely delicious in his all-black suit, hair pulled back into a simple loose bun. Though he probably refused her advances with gel or whatever shimmering clip she dared bring in his vicinity. His grey eyes shifted to mine, heating slightly as they took me in from head to toe.

"I wasn't intending to, but now I don't feel like being around people at all," he murmured. Then he bent, pressing his lips to my neck, "When you look like that, I can barely contain myself."

"Obviously," I murmured, sarcasm lacing my voice, but I still giggled. He groaned, straightening himself.

"Really, she was just being fussy. I don't know why I have the audacity to still be shocked, knowing her mother."

"Oh, is that so?" I arched a brow, gazing down to the little pearl bundle in his arms. "Were you being so fussy for daddy he had to go for a walk to calm down?"

Bright blue eyes beneath curly black hair peered up at me as I raised my daughter from his arms. Tickling her belly elicited the bubbling laughter from her that I loved so much. Teasingly, I went on, "Was daddy brooding while waiting for mommy to help him because we only listen to one another?" She giggled again, as if in affirmation.

"Rub it in, why don't ya?" He muttered, but there was a smile on his face. He leaned down again, pressing a gentle kiss to my lips this time before shifting to kiss the top of her head.

"Are you sure you're okay with doing this? I can march out there and tell my mom we want to wait," I offered, studying him. He sighed but shook his head.

"I'd rather get the public spectacle over with so we can go on with our lives." His eyes roved over me again as he added under his breath, "And so that I may publicly call you Governess whenever I wish, and not have to reserve that title for our bed."

"Fair." I grinned, and he fell into step beside me as we made our way back to the dining hall, using the main walkway this time. I paused in the doorway, already registering the hovering drones outside the window which had yet to see us.

Ax's arm immediately circled my shoulders, pulling me into a protective cocoon as I held our daughter to my chest. Looking down at her, I brushed that one stubborn lock of hair off her little forehead before whispering gently,

"You exist beside the flower, Anna.
Let's show everyone just how beautiful and
powerful we Thorne women can be."

<u>Acknowledgements</u>

As always, my first and biggest thank you will go to my wonderful husband. The extent of your patience and love never fails to shock me, and I will never be able to express how grateful I am for it. This book was exhausting for us both. The trauma it dug up, and the very real fear or anger I expressed while being completely wrapped up in the mindset of one of the characters, is something I am very lucky to not have to have gone through alone. You are my peace, my love.

I would also like to thank my wonderful beta readers, who dedicated several months of their time to whittle away at this project and help me perfect it. With some of the scenes, I know it couldn't have been easy. Thank you for supporting this story, and helping it flourish.

Last but certainly not least, I would like to thank my good friend Rey. You've been on the receiving end of more than one discord paragraph or phone call about this book (and many others) when I couldn't get my mind straight. Thank you for your love and support, and keeping my braincell alive through the tedious, and sometimes downright frustrating moments of being an indie author.

And to my glorious readers: thank you for your time and love. Your support keeps us writers going.

~Nightshade